T0064442

The Spice
of
London

The Spice
of
London

SM PATIBANDA

PARTRIDGE

A Penguin Random House Company

Print information available on the last page.

To order additional copies of this book, contact
Partridge India
000 800 10062 62
orders.india@partridgepublishing.com

www.partridgepublishing.com/india

CONTENTS

SALLY

His first contact with Sally was extraordinary. At the sight of him, she kicked him on the face with the dorsal of her foot, complete with the hip action and the scream. It was a Friday, and dry in September. The location was the bus station in Staines. He had been in London for four days. He came out of his residence for some fresh air and to stretch his legs. The time was 8:30 pm. Like everywhere in London, there were a few people in the bus station unlike his country, where all such places are filled with large crowds. The shops were closed. It happened near the door of Argos. There were no people. He saw Sally come out of the exit door of the mall.

Suddenly a young man emerged from the shadows, grabbed her handbag and tried to jerk it out of her hands. She kicked him hard on his chest. She missed his solar plexus. Another young man emerged from the shadows and tried to help his comrade. She had already kicked the first attacker off when his accomplice tried to help. She gave a reverse spinning kick. Her heel contacted the nape of the neck of the second attacker. Her handbag fell to the floor. Seeing that the woman was out numbered, he rushed to help her. Meanwhile, the attackers fled. When he reached her, she kicked him as described above.

He collapsed to the floor. Before he could realize what happened, three people waiting for the bus at the far end of the bus station came running to rescue her. The police arrived within a few minutes. They were courteous and spoke pleasantly. They glanced sternly at the man on the floor. They helped him to his feet and examined his face. The left side of his face was red. As she kicked him with her shoes on, the impact was hard, leaving a red stripe on his face. One eye was swollen.

She explained the incident to the police.

'I was in the high street of Staines. I wanted to go the car park. I came through the mall and came out of it into the bus stand. As soon as I came out at Argos, a man approached stealthily and grabbed my hand bag. I kicked him off. Before I could regain my balance another man jerked the bag out of my hands. I spun and kicked him. Seconds later this man came running to me. Both the attackers were of south Asian origin. When a third man from the same south Asian descent appeared, I assumed that he was part of the gang and kicked him in self- defence.'

The police officer who appeared to be senior of the two, said, 'I am Detective Inspector James Archibald. This is Assistant Inspector Mary Milton. Will you please accompany us to the police station? A crime was committed. We are glad that one of the gang was caught. We are not arresting anybody yet. We will find out what happened and take your statements. We will register a complaint and take necessary steps if we are convinced that there is a case. When we believe that further action is necessary, we will inform you. You can call your lawyer or others for help. For the present, it's only a preliminary enquiry.'

They got into the police car. Sally tried to call somebody on her mobile. Mary stopped her saying,

'Please do not call anybody. Please do not create a worrisome situation. You are the victim. Please don't panic.'

James Archibald threw a glance at his assistant and continued driving. They arrived at the police station and trooped into the Detective Inspector's office. Archibald called a paramedic and requested him to give the first aid and advise whether the injury was simple.

The paramedic scrutinized the face and said, 'The injury is light. There is a black eye. There is black stripe on left side of his face from the temple down to the jaw. He may also run high temperature tonight. He will be all right in a couple of days. He is strong, healthy and young.' He applied some ointment on the injured area and left.

Archibald told them, 'This is a simple case. I do not see any reason to deny help. I have changed my mind. You can call anybody you wish. I am expecting a call. Please go to the lobby or the reception.'

Sally had a cell phone. The young man did not call anybody.

When they returned to his cabin, they found Archibald talking on the phone. Sally whispered, 'He didn't even take our names. We have been with him for more than half an hour.'

Archibald finished his call and said, 'I have called for CCTV footage. It will be here in ten minutes. This is not an open and shut case. There was an attempt to rob a woman, and there was an assault on this person. With my experience in solving crime, I am convinced that this man is not a criminal. I am beginning to believe that you hastily attacked a man who came to your help.'

'I have the basis for my action. Both the attackers were coloured and were of the south Asian origin. When this man came running to me, I felt that he was part of the gang because he too was of the same south Asian descent. I assumed that he was part of the gang that attacked me'.

'Your explanation reeks of racism. You cannot presume his involvement in the crime because of his features.'

A knock on the door interrupted him. He said, 'Come in.'

A policeman entered carrying a delivery from the Pizza Hut.

Archibald said, 'I did not order a pizza.'

He looked at the young man incredulously and asked, 'You ordered a pizza?'

'No sir. I did not, even though I am hungry.'

'You should not order pizzas and other food when you are in police custody. Even though you are not under arrest, you are technically under our custody for questioning.. An opportunity is normally given to the suspects to call their lawyer or some help from the family or friends. You should not misuse it.'

'I do not have the telephone number of the people I am staying with. I know the address and will take you there if you accompany me.'

'You don't have the telephone number of the people you are living with, but know the telephone number of the Pizza Hut.'

'I don't know the number. I did not order it.'

The policeman said, 'The delivery man is waiting for the payment.'

He paid and said, 'The pizza will be too much for you. Let the three of us share it.'

'I don't want the pizza, I want to go home.' said Sally

'We will send you home shortly. We are trying to find out what happened and seek your cooperation. Did you call anybody?'

'I did. I called my mother. She is bringing a solicitor to help me in the matter.'

His assistant came and logged on to the computer. She turned the screen to enable Sally and the man to watch it.

She asked, 'I ordered a Pizza. I see that it is delivered. I thought you might be hungry.'

'Since when did you start caring about other people's hunger?'

'I thought that the Indian could be hungry. He is not in a position to order food.'

The incident was caught on two cameras. The footage showed clearly that the man came to help. He ignored the handbag on the floor. He was looking at Sally and was trying to see if he can be of any help to her. He did not move toward her. The culprits fled by the time he reached crime scene.

Sally said, 'I am sorry. In the heat of the moment I assumed that he was a member of the gang.'

Archibald said, 'Now give your bio data, finger prints and photographs. I am not asking for mug shots. Call your mother and tell her to go back and wait for you at home. Please report here at 9:30 am tomorrow and give your statements and complaints, if any.'

Both of them were dropped at their homes by a police man in plain clothes in an unmarked car. The police man spoke to the people living in the houses and confirmed that they were indeed living there.

Next day, they assembled in Archibald's cabin. Sally was accompanied by her mother and a Solicitor. The injured man was accompanied by a man of 45 years and he was angry. Archibald picked up a paper. He looked at the young man. He read aloud.

'You are Siva Kanuri, age 22 years. You are a graduate in Electronics Engineering. Arrived in London four days ago for higher studies in U K. I do not see any reason for studying further. You Indians and Chinese are obsessed with the educational qualifications. You are an engineer with software skills. You can get a job. Don't interrupt. That is only a comment. Not criticism. You are looking to move out in couple of days and are also looking for part time job.'

He picked up Sally's bio data.

'You are Sally Richard, also 22 years, daughter of late Harry Richard. You are a B.A, in English, enrolled in the Royal Holloway College in Egham for M.B.A. Both of you deny any history of violence, crime and conviction.'

Siva interrupted, 'I am a black belt in karate in the Budokai school of karate whose grand master was Gogen Yamaguchi. There was history of violence, but that was only sport.'

Archibald continued, 'Sally Richard too has no history of violence except that of yesterday. She is also trained in martial arts. You live with your mother.'

Her mother explained, 'I live with my daughter. I have one daughter and no other children. I have not remarried after my husband's death.'

'Why not ?'

'I am yet to meet a man who is close to the calibre and quality of Harry by half. I am not interested in others.'

'It is hard. I think that you are missing the good things in life. I know that it is none of my business and I am interfering. You are beautiful. You don't look like the mother of a twenty two year old. In a photo of you and your daughter together, it will be difficult to identify the mother.'

'Thank you.'

'When you talk about Harry, is he the billionaire Richard known for the chain of car show rooms across UK and Europe?'

'Yes.'

'It is a privilege to meet you lady. I would prefer to have met you in more pleasant circumstances.'

'My daughter is not at fault. She acted in self-defence.'

'She kicked an innocent and well-meaning man who came to her rescue. I have records of people who died for less severe attacks. A mere slap killed a man. CCTV footage shows clearly that the incident was over before Siva reached your daughter. She should have paused a second before kicking him. Her argument that the man is of the same ethnic group as the attackers is not tenable. That may land her in more trouble.'

'An inch above, the kick could have connected to his temple. He could have died. We are going to sue,' said Siva's guardian angrily.

Archibald said, 'We have the pictures of the culprits. We will circulate them and try to trace them. There is nothing to do until they are traced. You may leave. We will keep in touch.'

'What about us? We wish to sue her for the assault.'

'We will prosecute her if you complain. I advise you to be lenient. This is the first time she came in to the contact with the criminals. She stood her ground. I believe that she learned her lesson. She comes from a decent family and good upbringing. Your background is also decent. Both of you have no history of violence. While we do not know your background, I do not think that your ward is violent. That is my gut feeling. With my experience, I can smell a criminal a mile away. Please settle the matter amicably out of court.'

'I am surprised at your compassion for the girl. This boy suffered injury and anguish. There must be some sympathy for his situation too.'

'We have all the sympathy for him. Would he get justice if she goes to prison? She is twenty-two years old. There is the inexperience of youth.'

Sally's solicitor said, 'My client is not to blame. He was in the wrong place at the wrong time.'

'Once you go to court, you cannot predict how the judge would view the situation and interpret the law. You must have heard of the case in 2003 when a land lord shot the thief who broke into his house. The Judge convicted the land lord and sentenced him to prison. The thief was shot in the leg. That was reportedly the second time the thief broke into the house. Judges don't take physical assault lightly.'

Siva's guardian claimed, 'The injury may be small, but the offence is serious. She did not act with a criminal intent. No doubt, she acted according to her assessment of the situation. But the humiliation and agony suffered by him are greater than the physical injury.'

Archibald said, 'Siva and Sally better leave this room. Their presence is not needed now. They can wait outside. The negotiations will also be moved from my office. Everybody will leave my room within a few minutes.'

When Sally and Siva left the room, he said, 'Both of you agreed to not to pursue the matter in the court. Please come to an agreement soon. Please carry on your negotiations elsewhere. I suggested a solution to the problem. It is for you to sort it out. I do not want to be a party to it.'

'Thank you,' said Ms. Richard, 'I don't want the compensation to be high because I am rich. I do not throw away the hard earned money of my husband. Thanks again, for showing a way out,' and prepared to leave. Archibald got up from his seat and shook hands with everybody.

Siva is 6ft tall, well built and light in colour. Sally is white, 5'6" in height, attractive.

She said, 'I am sorry. I acted in haste and dangerously. I could have hurt your eye.'

'I was shocked when you kicked me. I am trained in martial arts too. Once my karate coach advised me that it is always cheaper and sensible to take a punch and leave it at that, than fight and incapacitate the opponent. You could get in to trouble with the law.'

'That is true. I am suspended by my karate school until this incident is sorted out.'

'Don't worry. It will end soon.'

'What is your telephone number?'

'The land line number is of no use as I am moving to another place soon. I do not have a mobile. Give me your number. I will call you as soon as I get one.'

'I will come to your place tomorrow. I will lend you a handset and a sim card. Return them as soon as you acquire your own set.'

'Thank you. You are very considerate.'

Siva's guardian, Mrs. Richard and the solicitor came out and joined them.

Siva's guardian said, 'We can continue the discussion at my house. It is only five minutes from here by walk.'

'You go ahead. We will join you in a few minutes. Sally knows the way,' said, Mrs Richard.

Siva and his guardian left for home.

The solicitor advised, 'We better quote an amount. We should not beat about the bush. Please name the amount that would be the minimum acceptable to you.'

She replied, 'That boy is decent and good-looking. I have no idea about the compensation. Once I quote an amount, I will stick to it and there will be no further negotiation.'

'There should be some flexibility. There are many lawyers and solicitors who will represent the boy and collect their fee from us after the case is won. They have a solid base. Let us negotiate.'

'I propose a compensation of ten grand.'

'Let us go to them and make the offer.'

Meanwhile, Siva's guardian spoke to Siva, 'I have no experience in negotiations of this kind. That woman is rich, but a hard nut to crack. Your injury is minor. I think that five grand would be adequate. You can repay a large portion of your education loan in India. We can consult a solicitor. He may negotiate a higher amount. I am not smart enough to extract large amount. I suggest that we take what they offer. That girl is decent and pretty. That is not the consideration for my advice.'

'I have no idea about these matters. I do not expect to become rich through this incident. Whatever you do is acceptable to me.'

After ten minutes, Sally and company arrived at Siva's residence and settled on the sofa. There was silence for some time.

Ms. Richard finally broke the silence and said, 'Determination of the cost of damage is difficult. People who are experienced in such matters can do it. As we have decided to settle the matter out of court, we should assess the damage ourselves. Since a solicitor is available, I took his advice. He did not make an elaborate assessment, but considered the amount quoted by me could be offered to you. You may get a much larger amount if you sue or you may not. As there was a physical assault, my daughter could get in to trouble. I am prepared to make an offer. I propose ten grand. I think that is fair and reasonable.'

Siva's guardian replied, 'We are not experienced in such matters either. We are not willing to make an issue out of this and haggle over the compensation. We are prepared to accept much lower amount. Since you made the offer, we accept it. Please have your solicitor draw up a document to be signed by my ward relinquishing all his rights in this matter.'

Mrs. Richard was immensely pleased. She said, 'I am delighted that you were quite frank and reasonable. I will send you the cheque and the document tomorrow. I wish Siva all the best.'

'Thank you. When we agreed for the settlement out of court, the major consideration was that your daughter had no criminal intent.'

They rose to leave. Sally stayed back for a few seconds. She handed him a mobile and said, 'You will find that all my contacts in its memory were deleted. You will find only my number in its memory. I can put the mobile on call divert, but calls for you will also be diverted. Please tell my contacts to call my mobile number given to you.'

'The education loan taken by me from the State Bank of India will be closed prematurely. I will be left with some surplus. Will you promise to kick me again next September?'

SIR ROBERT

Sally and Siva arrived at Sir Robert's villa in Osterly. The building is an old mansion renovated, refurbished and modernized. It faces a road 60ft wide. There is a large open ground suitable for soccer and rugby. Like all open places in London, the open ground is green with grass. Siva was impressed. 'Do people really live like the olden days when England was a great empire with rich colonies all over the globe,' asked Siva

Sally replied, 'I do not know. I very rarely meet the knights and noble families. Sir Robert and his wife are my mother's friends. I meet their family frequently because their daughter and I are class mates.'

'Your injury is healing rapidly. The traces of the injury will fade in a couple of days. You can seek a part time job. However, you are skilled in software. You better take a job that needs programming skills. Don't take up a job in a hurry. I think I can help. You can also get a full time job, but you have to get your visa category changed by the British Consulate in India.'

'I don't need a full time job. I want to complete my education here.'

'I will keep in touch with you. Meanwhile, apply for driving licence. I will take you to the University for admission.'

'Normally, when a new student is coming from India, the Indian students of the University get the information from the administrative office and contact him before he left India. They receive him at the airport and help him settle down. In my case I got a beautiful girl to help me'

'Flattering me will not get you anywhere. Don't get any ideas. I have a boyfriend. I will introduce you to him soon. You are only a friend. You are handsome, educated and intelligent. Almost all the girls of age of 20yrs and above have boyfriends. Besides you are too dark.'

'In India I am considered fair.'

'You may be the fairest in India but you are dark skinned. I am not being racist. You should know and adapt to the situations in U.K. You may make friends in the college. You should know the rules, let us not cross the limits. I like you. You have charm and pleasant manners.'

'Thank you for your frankness. However, we will keep in touch. I know my place now. I will not do anything to jeopardize our friendship. Wouldn't your boyfriend be jealous of your friendship with me.'

'No. Normally the girls do not cheat on their boyfriends. If they do, the relationship is in trouble and they may break up. I will not be jealous of your relationship with any girl.'

'I understand that the first step towards marriage is boy girl friendship. Second step is engagement and the third is marriage.'

'That is how it is more or less. There could be more than one boyfriend before a marriage is proposed. But the friendships are not simultaneous. The relationship would be broken before a relationship with a new boyfriend develops.'

'This is very difficult for the children. They have to fend for themselves and select their mates. Parents' help and guidance are desirable.'

'Parents don't interfere. It will be ignored or rejected even if it is attempted. It is tough on the adolescents. Tomorrow, I am taking you to Sir Robert. He is a PhD in biology. I do not know the details. I heard that you get a PhD if you discover a protein. He is the second son of a Lord. In UK the first son gets the farm and property. The other children have to find their own means of lively hood. His uncle became rich with successful business enterprises and died leaving all his property to Sir Robert.

He developed it and became richer than his uncle who did not marry and died a bachelor. Sir Robert is a businessperson and a scientist. In appreciation of his contribution to science, he was knighted in the same year, he won the Nobel Prize. He told me some time back that he needs a software developer.'

They stopped at the gate. There was a cabin at the gate manned by Security staff. They looked in to the car, recognized Sally and smiled. They waited for the gates to open. The gates were operated electrically.

They travelled about 100 yards on a black top road to reach the portico. A man came forward and opened door for Sally to get out. Siva got out of the car by himself. The man has taken the car for parking. They rang the bell.

The door was opened in a few seconds by the butler, who greeted Sally pleasantly and said, 'Sir Robert is expecting you. He is in the lab. Please follow me,'

He smiled at Siva. He took them to the lab on the second floor, which was reached by a lift. He entered the lab and announced, 'Sally and Siva' and closed the door behind him softly. Sir Robert was tall, slim with a radiant smile. Siva attributed the radiance to the smile of welcome. Siva was relieved by the smile. He was awe struck by the title, the butler and the valet.

'It is a great privilege to meet you Sir Robert. Please forgive me if I do not address you properly. I never imagined a meeting with a Knight. You have my respect and awe.'

'Relax, Siva, I am proud of my doctorate titles than the Knighthood.' said Sir Robert. He hugged Sally and kissed her on both the cheeks. Sally did likewise.

'He is from India landed in London one week back. Mom must have spoken to you about him.'

'She did. You are a graduate engineer with software skills. I can use you.'

'The software skills I possess are acquired by training. I have no experience. I can design a web site given an opportunity. I think I can develop software required, but I have not done any work in that direction. I can study the project and try to develop the required software.'

The butler entered the room silently carrying a tray with tea and biscuits.

He addressed Siva, 'Do you take some tea? If not we will serve you whatever you need'.

'Tea will be fine sir, can I have some sugar and milk.'

'In a few minutes, sir. I am not a big lord. I am his Lordship's servant. Please do not call me "Sir." You should address his lordship as "Sir" and address his wife as Lady Katherine.'

'That is enough James. He is new to the country and will learn the local customs soon,' said Sir Robert. Sir Robert is about 40 years old, with thin hair on his scalp, oval face with a dimple on the right cheek and magnetic charm.

'Siva you can relax and feel free. We are not formal. Formalities make life difficult. Let us see what we can do with you. At the university, I have associate professors and research assistants. I have a secretary provided by the university. I really do not know how you can be of any help here. You are here on a student visa, I suppose.'

'Yes sir. There is a limit to the number of hours per week I can work. We will confine to it. You are specialist in biology. I know nothing about it.'

'I am an engineer in genetics. I develop new technology and produce genetically modified life. We are yet to apply my research to humans. You know, what new technology can produce?'

'Yes sir. I can understand the technology. You alter the molecular structure of organic life to produce living beings as required. I think it is also called Nano technology. But, such new technology is at present applied to produce genetically modified seeds, medicines etc.,. I do not understand and approve of applying terms like Nano to engineering products. There are improvements and inventions but not new technology as you use in biology.'

'That is good. You have an opinion. That means that you studied and analysed in your own way. Your opinion may be wrong. It can be corrected when more information is available.'

Lady Kat entered the room. She hugged Sally, touched her cheeks with Sally's cheeks. She looked at Siva and said "Hello", and smiled. Siva jumped to his feet and stood straight and mumbled, 'It is an honour to meet you Lady.'

She noticed his nervousness and said, 'Take it easy young man. We do not eat humans here.'

'I never spoke to a foreigner in India until I boarded the plane to London. Now that I am here, I am a foreigner and dark skinned. I am aware that I am yet to learn the British etiquette and manners. I am nervous.'

'We have grown out of this colour stuff. Haven't we, Sally. The person matters. I am confused that you have become colour conscious in the first week of your stay in London. There must be about 15% of the population who discriminate a person by his colour. There will always be such people.'

'He is not to be blamed. It is my fault when I resisted the attempted robbery by snatching my handbag. I kicked Siva who came to my rescue because he is of the same origin as the attackers. On the way here, I raised the colour topic not as a racist comment, but as a situation prevailing in our society at present. He will grow out of it soon,' replied Sally.

Siva whispered something in to Sally's ear. Lady Kat observed it and asked Sally what it was about.

'Siva says that you are a stunning beauty, Lady Kat. He says that we should have guessed that a man of Sir Robert's intellect and calibre will not select an ordinary mortal and that you are a fairy.'

Sir Robert intervened saying, 'Do not spoil her please. I have to live with her.'

The atmosphere became informal, pleasant and cordial.

Siva said, 'My comment is spontaneous. It came out without effort. I would not dare flatter her at first sight.'

Lady Kat was pleased immensely.

'People have been seeing me for years and they are used to me. They don't pay such complements. They take my beauty for granted.'

The butler entered with a tray of tea. Lady Kate introduced. 'Mr. Siva, this is James, the butler. I don't know what we would have done without him. James, this is Siva.'

'I had the pleasure of escorting him in to the house a few minutes back Lady.'

'That is not enough Mr. Siva is a friend of Ms. Sally. He is educated and came to London to study space technology. You will see more of him.'

'It is very nice to meet you, Mr. Siva. I look forward to meeting you more often.'

Sir Robert said, 'Siva is discussing Nano technology. He doesn't approve of the use of the word in mechanical, metallurgical and engineering fields.'

Siva said, 'If they could convert lead into gold by altering its molecular structure, they can apply the term. Otherwise, it is alchemy.'

'Do you have opinion on the space technology?'

'Yes sir, Man dreamed first and achieved the dream through research and experiment. In the 15th century, travel by sea was considered hazardous, but men travelled by sea and discovered new lands and people. I give credit to Europeans for their spirit of adventure, invention of tools and weapons and war fare.'

'Where does it take us?'

'It has enabled them to achieve the dream and explore the exotic places and dominate the globe. They explored everything that was possible in the world of three dimensions. The other dimensions exist and have to be explored.'

'I think that you are straying into fantasy.'

'No sir, I think that man is a prisoner of three dimensions. He can see and explore his world. In matters relating to space, things are complicated. The cosmic distances and time scales are beyond the reach of mankind.'

'Why do you say that?'

"The nearest earth like planet is 643 light years away. If man travels at 186,000 miles per second, which is the speed of light. He reaches that planet in 643 years. Man will not reach the planet during his life time.'

'You are beginning to make sense. Go on.'

'Man cannot travel at the speed of light. He will not survive that speed. Already an entrepreneur is selling tickets for a tour of Mars. The tour will travel at a speed of 2000 miles per hour. It takes two years to reach Mars, stay on Mars for two years and the return journey is another two years. They need provisions for six years. The satellite should be as big as a cruise ship. Recycling of excretion etc., are considered but after recycling twice, the nutrition will be nil. But I think that he will succeed.'

'The ancient Hindus visualized the cosmic distances and time scales. What did they suggest?'

'I am surprised and pleased that you are aware of the ancient cosmic concepts of the Hindus. The Hindu culture started losing dominance since the fourteenth century. The Sages said that you can cover the cosmic distances if you travel at the speed of the mind. That doesn't solve our problem.'

'What do you suggest?'

'We return to fantasy. The fairies of the Greek and other classics could exist in other multi dimensions of four and above. The Hindu mythology consists of Yaksha, Gandharva, Kinnera and other creatures who travel between stars and galaxies in no time. They do not appear to have the cosmic distances in their dimensions. They must be living in dimensions more than three. Man should visualize those dimensions and create a carrier in the multidimensional world. That carrier should be able to transport the 3D creatures to other planets. I am quite confident that we will achieve it.'

'I am glad that I stayed to listen to your assessment of the space travel. Will you take some more tea,' asked Lady Katherine.

Sally said 'wow' and smiled

Sir Robert said, 'I think you can be useful to me. You are employed. As you established instant rapport with Kat, I think, we can put you up in our house. Let me talk to James. One more mouth to feed is no problem.'

'You have a very big house hold. The salaries alone must come to two grand per month. Don't you feel it difficult to maintain such a large house.'

'It is not good manners to talk about a man's finances and source of income. You will learn soon enough. As you have already asked, I will explain. I take business decisions. Kat takes care of the business management. She is successful. We don't manage the companies. The day to day affairs and management are taken care of by the professional managers. We appoint the Auditors who report to us. We also get monthly performance reports. We are comfortable in money matters.'

He was glad to explain the success of his businesses. His acquaintances and friends never ask. He wanted to talk about his businesses, but felt that others may be bored

'You are calling her Kat not her ladyship or Lady Kat?'

'She is my wife, man. She was Kat before I became a Knight. Besides, we are quite informal here. You can sense that. I have answered your doubts about my finances. Kat and I were friends since our nursery school.'

'I am sorry.'

'That is alright. But be careful with James. He will not stand it and will give you a sermon at first opportunity. He is loyal. He had been in our family since my birth. He was my employee years before my knight hood.'

'As I am your employee now, I would like to take a look at your computer.'

'The computerization has been a pain since it needs a password stored in your brain. The modern day needs a lot of numbers. There is telephone number, pin number for your debit and credit cards, the card numbers and so on. Therefore, I lock my pc with a password. You have to use the pass word to log in. Some files have separate passwords. The pc password is used first thing in the morning and the access is open.'

'People are using tablets, laptops etc. you are still using a pc.'

'This is a standalone pc and is not portable. I have access to several data files in the University. I do not use the laptop or tablet while on the move. I use the pc here and at the office.'

Lady Kat and Sally were listening to the conversation.

Siva sat before the pc and moved the mouse. The Windows "start" screen appeared. He studied the icons. Most of them relate to biology and genetics.

'I have no knowledge of biology and genetics. Most of the icons relate to these topics, I wonder if you are wasting your money on me. What is the icon "organs".

'I will open it,' he opened it.

Siva turned away while Sir Robert entered his password.

Sir Robert explained, 'I am a Trustee of St. John's organ bank. We procure the human organs donated by the deceased and supply them to the needy through an established hospital. We collect the expenses. The organ is given free. The organization should declare a small loss, which will be made up by the trustees. That is legitimate organisation. We do not steal the organs.'

'Why did you log in to the file on 23rd Aug, spend 36 minutes and did nothing. Those 36 minutes had no activity.' asked Siva.

'I did not log into the file on 23rd Aug or any other date during the last one year.'

'You opened the file. Let me print the activity log. Yes. You logged in at 3:30 pm on 23rd.. Nobody used the file that day or several weeks before that date.'

'I do not know anything about it.'

'Were you at work that day?'

'Yes.'

"Somebody hacked into that website. They used it for some time and deleted the activity.'

'What do they gain by hacking the file?'

'You are dealing in human organs and there must be black market. The hacker is not from London.'

'A crime is committed or is contemplated. Can you retrieve any deleted matter?'

'Yes I am trying. Ah! You placed an enquiry for a human heart and kidney.'

'I did nothing of the sort.'

'There was a response from a Govt. Hospital in Panama.'

'What could be the purpose of their deal? Both the parties involved are genuine organizations who are not involved in shady deals,' asked lady Kat.

'There was another activity on 3rd September. Your organization had placed the order and the invoice was mailed. They must have taken a print out before deleting the transaction.'

'They have necessary papers to transport the organ to UK. Everything appears to be straight forward. You are being dragged into organ trafficking. There is something fishy and illegitimate.'

'We must stop this thing. We do not know what the hackers contemplate. The Organisation's activity is dormant. I am going to be a victim of fraud. That will be scandalous. The government may prosecute me. I may never go to St. John's. Now that we have discovered it. We should report it to the police. I may not be believed if I plead innocence after the discovery of fraud. My reputation will be ruined. I may eventually be proved not guilty, but the damage will be done.'

'Your organization is quite legitimate in its operations. We should treat this as extremely confidential. It should stay with the four of us.'

'I want to complain to the police, I cannot handle it without the knowledge and the support of police.'

'Of course, we will report to the police. We are neither competent nor capable of investigation. We will copy the required material in to a disc. We should not visit this page. We may alert the criminals. You should not get mixed up in this activity. We should complain to the police, It should be confidential.'

'So, how should we go about it?'

Sally intervened and said, 'Siva, I have seen you meeting Mary, the Asst. Inspector of Police. You were both seen together in the Starbucks. I don't know if you are dating, but you were quite close to be called her friend. You can report this matter through her.'

'I am not dating her. It is very difficult to find girls like her. Mary is the right choice. I will talk to her. I am a stranger to the city. I may not arouse any suspicion.'

Sir Robert said, 'Siva you must move into our house. We will provide suitable accommodation. As for food, it may not cost much because you can share the food with us. We must be throwing away the surplus food daily.'

He rang the bell and when James glided in. 'James Siva here will be moving into our house. Please provide him the necessary lodge and board. He is educated and is of great use to me,' said Sir Robert.

'I will allot him a comfortable room in our quarters.'

'Can't you accommodate him in the bed room available in our floor.'

'That will not be proper sir, he is not an equal.'

'That is racist James,' protested Sir Robert'

'No sir. Even in his own country, he will not be equal to the family of your standing. He is not a guest. He is an employee. So, he sleeps in our quarters.'

Siva said, 'He is right, Sir Robert. I will be at ease in quarters allotted by James. I need help in adjusting to the British etiquette and manners. I will move in in a couple of days.'

He returned to Staines with Sally. He rang up Mary and asked her to meet him at the Subway at 5:30 pm. Mary suggested that they could meet in her home, which is on the first floor of a semi detached house in Richmond. She has taken the entire first floor of the house. The ground floor is shared by three students.'

He had visited her house earlier. Normally they meet at Starbucks or an Indian restaurant in Staines. They became intimate. They liked each other. They slept together a couple of times. They realised that it was not possible to develop in to a permanent relationship and stopped indulging in sex.

Siva said, 'I want to talk to you in confidence.'

'You wanted to meet me to talk?'

There was curiosity in the voice.

'What is bothering you?'

'It is about Sir Robert. He is becoming a victim of a criminal conspiracy. The perpetrators are not framing him intentionally, but he is becoming a pawn in their diabolic scheme.'

'What do you want me to do? It is not in my jurisdiction.'

'I will give you some information. Please pass it on to the concerned officials. Sir Robert will cooperate with you.'

'What is all this about?'

Siva explained the situation.

She said, 'This could be a case of trafficking in human organs or could be a case of drug smuggling. I will pass on this intelligence to the competent authority. I may get some credit for this Are you leaving? Have some tea or coffee and some cakes'

'Not today. I am moving house. I may not see you again until this is sorted out. I will be in constant touch until this case is closed. We shall celebrate next week.'

'You think it will be so soon.'

'They don't hack in to the organization and wait unnecessarily. They will create the necessary papers and proceed with their diabolic scheme.'

'You are right. Sir Roberts's organization is legitimate. With their local standing, they cannot risk a scandal and trouble with the law.' They spoke for a few more minutes and Siva prepared to leave.

'I will see you again next week.'

He returned to Sir Robert's villa with his personal belongings. His guardian saw to that he packed his belongings and saw him off. He hired a cab and arrived at his new home.

James showed him to his room. It is quite large and has an attached toilet. It was furnished with a bed, a large study table and a chair. There is another chair with cushions with reclining back.

James said, 'Now that you are settled comfortably, let me make some things clear. In this floor, you do not have to be formal.. Don't address anybody "Sir", There will always be some surplus food. Feeding one more mouth will not be a burden. You will be woken up at 6:00 am with bed coffee. You will have breakfast with us. You make friends with Beth, the cook and you can have breakfast in bed. She is my wife.'

'Thank you.'

'I don't know what you did, but Lady Katherine is thoroughly impressed with you. She is anxious that you should be comfortable.'

'She is very kind.'

'Yes. Sir Robert is also interested in you. He still feels that you should be accommodated as a guest. Let us go to the kitchen. I will introduce you to the other staff. There is a separate door to enter and leave the premises exclusively by the staff.'

The kitchen is very large. There is space for dinning. Beth, Bessy and Jenifer were busy doing their chores. They welcomed him with smiles. The male servants are busy outside. You can meet them during the dinner. You want a drink?'

'You mean liquor? I don't drink. Coffee or tea will be ok.'

"That will be arranged. Don't call me for any service. You go to the kitchen and ask Beth or the other maids. You can help yourself if you do not come in their way. Now you help yourself for your cup of tea.

CARLOS GONSALVES

Carlos Gonsalves is 21 years old. He finished school. He did not go to college as he could not afford it. His parents have six children, of which three are girls. He is number four in the family. After school, he enrolled for a career in football.. After one year, the coach told him that he had no talent and aptitude for the game. He was advised to seek other options. He chose boxing, but that was also considered not suitable. He is well built and handsome. His enthusiasm for football and boxing gave him a supple, strong body and he kept it that way.

He left his native place and moved to Mexico City. He took up a job as a Teller in a Savings And Loans Bank. He met Margarita in the bank when she approached it for a loan. They dated for about six months. Carlos proposed and Margarita accepted. They were engaged after two days. They intended to marry one year later.

They consulted several event managers for the wedding. They found that selecting life partner is nothing compared to the cost of marriage. They were disappointed and frustrated. One day, he received a phone call from Senorita Augusta. She requested him to meet her at a restaurant near his place of work at 6:00 pm.

He went to the restaurant and asked the bartender if there was any reservation of a table. The bartender enquired about his name and showed him a table. He ordered tequila and waited. After a few minutes, a well-dressed pretty woman arrived and sat at his table.

She asked, 'You are Carlos Gonsalves I presume.'

'Yes.'

'You are badly in need of money, right?'

'Who isn't?'

'May be everybody does. But are you willing to work for it?'

'Yes.'

'We have a job for you.'

'How did you know about me?'

'We have scouts, who search for frustrated people in need of money or other favours. The scout reported that you are in need of money.'

'What should I do?'

'The job is that you should deliver a package to a customer in London. Once the delivery is made, you are discharged.'

'What is the catch?'

'You should not have asked. As you are taking the risk, you better know. You have to accompany a consignment to London. Your remuneration is $50,000.'

'I deliver a box and my job is over. It appears to be easy and simple. Where is the catch?'

'The consignment is human organs. While every effort is made to make the deal legitimate, things may go wrong, you could be arrested. You may spend about one to two years in jail. The compensation will be attractive'

'If you make a mistake, I go to jail. I don't want to get involved in anything illegal.'

'You will be paid $20,000 in advance and the balance after the job is done. If you are caught, we will pay the balance to your nominee. We will also pay the legal expenses for your defence in the trial.'

'That sounds appealing. How can I trust you?'

'That is the policy of the bosses. The field operatives are called assets or soldiers. The Syndicate takes care of its soldiers. They are not abandoned. If an operative dies in duty, his family is compensated adequately and paid pension. They have set up a legitimate pension fund. That will keep the soldiers loyal, disciplined and willing to risk their lives.'

'The proposal is attractive. Why me?'

'You are clean. No conviction for crime, violence and you are an honest worker'

'When do I start?'

'Three days from now. Please give us your passport, the details of your work experience etc.'

'When do you pay me the advance?'

'As soon as we get your visa'

'Alright. I will give my passport in an hour. I have to go home to pick it up.'

'I will come with you. I will wait outside in the car while you go in and fetch the passport. The visa is only for three days. You will have tickets to and fro and hotel reservations.'

Two days later, Augusta called him to collect the passport from the bartender at the restaurant.

The bartender handed him a large envelope and a brief case. He went home, Augusta called him and told him that the consignment is ready and it will be handed over to him at the Panama City airport.

He called Margarita and asked her to wait for him. He arrived at her place at 7:30 pm.

He handed her the brief case and told her, 'The briefcase contains $20,000, If I do not return, please keep the money. That is for you. If I get in to trouble, they will pay $30,000 which shall be given to my parents. If I return safely I keep the entire amount. Please arrange for my defence in court if required. The Syndicate pays the money. If I am convicted and sentenced for long time, please keep the $20,000 and spend it for your needs and find another man to marry.'

When he met Augusta the next day, he told her, 'In case I am questioned and tried for any crime by court, my defence may be handled by my fiancé, Margarita. The balance $30,000 may please be paid to my parents.'

Augusta acknowledged his nomination and said, 'If you are arrested and interrogated, do not try to be a hero. Sing.'

'What is there to sing? I know nothing.'

'It is safer that way. You follow their instructions, the Syndicate will support you. If you deviate, you are on your own. The Syndicate expects loyalty from you. They don't kill people like in the movies. The soldier is treated as an indispensable asset. They tolerate unavoidable and genuine mistakes. When it comes to their security, they are ruthless.'

'The large envelope contained the tickets, the passport, the hotel reservation and cash for the expenses. He has to go to Panama City to collect the consignment. Somebody will meet him at the airport and hand over the consignment.

He waited at the portico of the airport. After some time, an ambulance arrived and dropped a man and a vertical long box. The man looked around located Carlos and moved towards him. The consignment was similar to the water dispenser, but slightly bigger and has wheels. The man handed him the box and some papers and paid money for two airlines to keep the box refrigerated in transit and a packet of disposable gloves.

The man said, 'Your plane will land at Heathrow airport. Do not take the green channel, but declare the consignment to the airport customs. Have a nice trip,' and left.

Carlos examined the documents. They are invoice by the Panama City organ bank in favour of St. John's organ bank in London, certificate of origin, another certificate that the consignment contains genuine human organs donated by a deceased donor etc., and a key to the box.

Augusta came up to him and smiled.

She asked, 'Are you satisfied with the documents?'

'This operation appears to be in order.'

'The box will be redirected to another destination as the St. John's has ordered the organs for transplantation to a patient in another hospital. Somebody will meet you at the airport to collect the box. If after reasonable time nobody approaches you, please go to the hotel. It will be collected there. After checking in to the hotel, take a leisurely bath and await a representative of the consignee.'

'You seem to be very well informed about the Syndicate.'

'No. I never met any representative of the Syndicate. I am paid well for my services. I get my instructions from anonymous sources. My name is not Augusta. I was named after the month in which their plot was hatched. We will never meet again. Best of luck.'

In the airport at the Panama City, he passed the security check and the scan. They examined the document and asked him to open the box. He opened and stared at the contents. There were two glass partitions covered by ice cubes and frozen in the compartments. The upper portion contained sterile glass containers and the lower portion has a compressor and a battery, which keep the contents frozen. The upper portion has two walls. There was a gap between the outer and inner walls. The gap was filled with ice cubes.

The security officer wanted to separate the cubes and look at the tight glass containers. Carlos hesitated for a second, as he had no instructions in the matter. But as the request was official, he put on a pair of disposable gloves, and separated the ice cubes. There was a heart and a kidney in the glass cubicles. He was cleared. He wanted to be present when the container is loaded into the cargo bay, but the airline did not allow him.

In London, the Customs authorities were waiting for such cargo for the last seven days following St. John's complaint. If the cargo was prima facie in order but for the forged documents of St. John's and the Panama City organ bank, they would allow the transporter to leave and shadow him to the destination in London. Carlos landed in London, collected his luggage and cargo after getting his passport stamped and walked towards the customs. He was surprised at the speed and eagerness with which the Customs Authorities received him. They verified the documents, which were perfect. If they had not known about the fake papers of the organ banks, they would have cleared him. A doctor of the forensic laboratory was summoned. He looked at the organs and confirmed that they were genuine and human.

The Customs Officer apologized and said, 'Sorry, we kept you waiting. You know that there is a large trade in species and human organs. We cannot take things lightly. You may go.'

Relieved, Carlos waited at the exit gate. When nobody came forward to meet him for half an hour, he turned around walked towards the hotel through the passage that led to the Reception Desk of the hotel from the airport terminal. It was 7 PM when he checked into his room, As instructed, he poured himself a drink and had gone to the toilet for a leisurely shower and rest. As the airlines fed him throughout his journey, he was not hungry.

The Customs Officials were perplexed. They allowed Carlos to leave, hoping to catch the next person in the line and then the third person and so on. They reported to the Chief Customs Officer and discussed the situation.

The Chief said, 'It is odd that they brought human organs all the way from Panama with forged documents. The organs were genuine. They forged the indent and invoice. The certificates from the labs regarding the blood group and other documents will no doubt be genuine.'

'May be they killed a man for these organs,' suggested an Officer

'That is possible. The market for human organs is big, no doubt. But it is unusual to kill a man and transport the organs across the continents. They can procure the organs by killing a man locally and avoid the Customs. We better rope in the Drugs and Narcotics Control personnel,' said the Chief.

The Chief suddenly exclaimed, 'It's the drugs no doubt. I am surprised that no one in this Department had considered this angle.'

When they contacted the Narcotics Division, they enquired about the sniffer dogs. The Customs Official replied that the dogs were of no use as they were confused by the scent of the organs.

The Official in the Narcotics said, 'They are smuggling the Drugs. Siege the container and arrest the man. We will be there in a few minutes.'

The customs personnel rushed to the hotel and took possession of the container and arrested the man in the toilet who was naked and covered by the foam of soap. They seized the lift and the stairs. They missed narrowly, the two persons, one of whom was carrying a duffel bag. They examined the container thoroughly. It had two walls all around. The gap between the two walls was filled with ice cubes. The walls under the upper chambers were deceptively concealed and was difficult to open. When they opened it finally, it was vacant. There was nothing inside.

The Narcotics man sad, 'They are packing the high purity Cocaine or Heroin in hundred gram sachets. This chamber underneath can accommodate ten packets per row and ten packets per column. That is ten thousand grams. Ten kgs of narcotic drug was successfully smuggled in to U.K.. It will hit the streets in an hour.'

When weighed the container again, It was 10 kgs lighter. Carlos was indicted on two counts, one for illegal trafficking of human organs and another, for smuggling Narcotics. The CCTV cameras were of no help as the two men had taken great care to avoid exposure to the cameras. The Police interrogated Carlos for one day. On the second day they produced him before a Judge, who remanded him to custody in Her Majesty's prison. He declined the offer of a telephone call and also the help of an attorney. The investigating Officials tried to persuade him to call for help.

He did not want to expose Margarita to the Police in this case. The Police realized that Carlos was merely a courier. As expected, he did not have any information with him. But he brought human organs to London illegally. He was likely to be sentenced to six months to two years on the first count and three to five years for smuggling narcotics. On the evening of the second day, Margarita visited him. She explained to him the situation and told him that a high profile Lawyer was hired to defend him.

He asked, 'What is his name?'

She said, 'Ruth Crawford. If Ruth Crawford could not get you acquitted, nobody else can.'

She also assured him that she would be in London until the trial is over and visit him as many times as the prison rules permit.

PAUL BLAKE

*E*ddie Lazarus suffered heart stroke while in prison. He was moved to the prison hospital. He spoke to his cell mate Perry Burn who was permitted to visit him.

'I may not survive this stroke. Even if I do survive and is released on parole, I think that I cannot complete a few domestic chores, I need help. I know that you are honest and trustworthy. You are likely to be released in a few months, will you help?'

Perry asked, 'I sure, will. But how can you trust me? I am in prison. I am a convict. Honest person with integrity doesn't come here.'

'I know why you are here. You gave shelter to a fugitive, because he was a friend.'

'Yes, that was stupid of me. My wife and children were at her mother's place. I could not turn him away even though he told me that he murdered a man out of jealousy. He was with me for three days and left when my family was coming back. I was treated as accessory after the fact. When he was interrogated by the police, he confessed to crime, he also gave the information regarding the cooperation he received as a fugitive. I was convicted and sentenced to four years in jail.'

'That is exactly the reason why I trust you. You helped a friend in distress. Everybody confesses during police interrogation. They know the truth even though they cannot get a conviction in the court. I am serving time here for a crime. I deserve to be in jail.'

'Why are you here?'

'I was accused of robbery and assault. I was identified by the victim in a line up. He testified in the court that it was me that assaulted him.

He could not see well as it was dark and the CCTV footage was also not clear. The victim was in error. I had iron clad alibi.'

'Why did you not use it?'

'For the crime I did not commit the sentence could be 4 years in jail. For the alibi, I could not use, I could be sentenced to 5 to 7 years. I was glad to be convicted for assault and robbery.'

'What was the crime?'

'I was in the vault of the London Metropolitan Bank's Main branch. The heist was successful. They never caught the culprits.'

'How many were involved and what did you do with the booty?'

'There were only two of us. The larger the team, the more is the risk of somebody committing a mistake affecting the whole team. Look. I am confiding all this to you on the belief that you would keep this confidential at any cost.'

'I swear. Tell me about the bank robbery. It is fantastic.'

'The bank had elaborate, electronic security arrangements in place. I can operate the security systems and menu driven software. We succeeded in beating them. Inside the vault, we did not touch the cash or gold bricks. We went for the diamonds. Holding large amounts of cash or gold is risky. My accomplice is an expert in breaking open the safes. He is an artist in that line. We went for the diamonds because, they are easy to carry and can be converted to cash when needed. He had a principle. He would commit only one crime in his life that will take care of his family for generations. If he fails in his first attempt, he will not attempt it again. We will discuss the matter in detail later. He opened a cloth bag and poured the contents of it on to his palm and closed his palm. He closed the cloth bag and tied the mouth of the bag. Later, when we counted there were 108 diamonds of various carats. I don't know much about the diamonds. He told me that they are pure and would be very valuable. He divided the contents in to three parts. There were two mounds of fifty diamonds each and one small mound of eight diamonds. He explained that an employee of the Security System Company had to be paid two million pounds for supplying copies of the security designs. He will be paid in diamonds. If he is not in a hurry, he will get more than two million pounds. The minimum value in a distress sale will be more than two million pounds. He gets a large bonus.'

I told him, 'I want my share. After taking my share, I don't want to see you again in my life. He said that one has to liberal in payment of remuneration. He gave me fifty diamonds.'

'Thank you. You are giving me fifty percent of the loot.'

'Don't think your contribution is small. Without you, I could not have gone in to the vault. You are the most important person in this adventure. Don't call this treasure a loot.'

'I divided my share in to five packets and hid them at five different locations in London. I was arrested minutes after I stashed away the last of the bags.'

'Great. Are they still there?'

'They should be. Even if one or two of them are missing, others may be there. If I do not survive this heart attack, please give fifty percent of the stash to my wife. She works as a waitress in a restaurant. I could not make any arrangements for her financial needs. Take the other fifty percent as your compensation.'

'O.K., Best of luck.'

Eddie returned to his cell after a few days. He gave the locations to Perry. Two months later, Eddie was released from jail as the real culprit, was caught in the investigation of another crime that would get him a sentence of 30 years. He confessed to the robbery that put Eddie in jail. He admitted in court that an innocent person is serving time for the crime committed by him.

Before leaving the prison, Eddie gave him his address and contact number.

He said, 'Perry, I am not going in search of my treasure as I don't want to lead anybody following me to the diamonds. The Insurance Company may still be pursuing the case. Please collect the ice after your release and deliver them to me.'

The jail authorities have taken special interest in Eddie's case and have arranged for a grant from the government to rehabilitate him. Three days after his release, the Probation officer visited Eddie at his house and discussed various proposals with him. Eddie's wife was present at the time.

She said, 'I don't like the idea of employment. I want him to set up his own business. It may be small. I don't think we can do business with large investment.'

'What do you have in mind?', asked the officer.'

'I think that a fish and chips stall is a good idea. People need food every few hours. We can start in a small scale. Initially we will set up a take away service. I think we can handle the business as I am experienced in that line as a waitress.'

'That is a good idea. Look for an ideal location. I will arrange the funds.' One week later Eddie's Fish &Chips was opened. In addition to fish & chips, they sold sausages, ice cream, soft drinks, water bottles, fruit juices etc. The location was so good that it was attracting customers in large numbers. The business was a hit. Eddie visited Perry at the prison and offered him employment when he comes out.

Perry said, 'Regarding the matter you confided in me, I have made arrangements with a close friend of mine to recover the material from their hidden locations and give them to you. His name is Paul Blake.'

Eddie was very angry. He was livid with rage.

Yet, he whispered, 'You have betrayed my trust. You have endangered my life and put me at the risk of losing my money.'

'Relax. Don't worry. You will be safe and so is your money. You will find that he is reliable and can be useful to you.'

'You can't trust anybody in that line of activity.'

'You will get the goods after the morning session is over. Keep the goods safely stashed away. Do not try to change the diamonds in to cash. I know a reliable fence. I will arrange to sell them. My advice to you is do not sell them in a lump sum. Sell one piece and spend it frugally. You will not get the market price. The fence will buy at a very low price. His profit margin will be high but he is good and safe. Don't worry about Paul Blake. He is a thief, but an honest one.'

Eddie's wife commented 'UK is said to be a developed country. More than 65% of its population do not get two square meals a day.'

'What do you mean?'

'People have to report for work by 9.00 A.M. They grab a couple of slices of bread and some coffee or whatever is available and rush to the bus or local train. They eat a burger or some thing light. Some physical fitness fads use their lunch time to jog. The full meal they have is dinner. There is a need. We can try to cater to that.'

'What would I have done without you.'

'You would have committed crime. Even with me as your wife, you committed crime.'

She does not know the story of the diamonds. They started Eddie's Breakfast.

There were two kinds of breakfast. Medium and Large. Breakfast was sold in foil packs. Medium pack consisted of two fried eggs, baked beans and toast with butter or jam or both spread. It was priced 1.99 pounds. It is difficult to eat it in the train during the peak hours. They can have it in the office. Large consisted of the contents the medium pack plus ham sausages, steak and some sea food. It was priced at 3.99 pounds. Lunch packets were also sold. They consisted of fish and chips and a dessert. It was priced at 4.99 pounds. The menu is changed daily. There was no breakfast on Saturday and Sundays.

They were getting bulk orders for breakfast and lunch. They were delivered by Siva. They had to take permission from the competent authority to open early and stay open till late in the evening. They employed staff to work in shifts. The business was so good that they were unable to cope up with it. They wanted partners. Three days later a handsome young man entered Eddy's restaurant at 11.30 AM and asked for Eddie Lazarus..'

'I am Eddie Lazarus. What can I do for you?'

'My name is Paul Blake. Perry Burn sent me.'

Lazarus looked into his eyes seriously and asked him to come into the room at the back. He asked his wife and the helper to leave them alone for a few minutes.

After they left the room, he said 'well.'

'I have the material in my possession. Where do you want it delivered?'

'Right here'

Paul pulled out five cloth bags and handed them over. Eddie opened all of them and emptied

He asked, 'You have not taken a single diamond?'

'No, I am a petty thief. Diamonds are too big for me. I cannot handle them. Perry offered me two diamonds. That will be enough for me.'

'I am glad that I met you, How old are you?'

'Twenty.'

'Finished school?'

'No, I dropped out.'

'I will help you finish your school. I will give you a job and finance your education. I have just discovered the joy of living straight. You should acquire enough skills to be employed gainfully.'

'I will try', replied Paul and stood up to leave.

'Please keep in touch. You have a job ready for you, whenever you want it. Best of luck,' said Eddie.

He visited Perry and told him that he received the material.

He told him, 'Our business is going by leaps and bounds. We are not able to handle it. I need a partner. I offer the partnership to you. I can't trust anybody else.'

Perry said, 'That is wonderful. But I won't be free for another two months.'

'How about your wife?'

'She is working as a clerk in a Law firm. Tell her to meet me. I will ask her to take up your offer. Having been in firm of lawyers, she doesn't trust anybody. She will insist on a fool proof agreement.'

'That is OK. That will protect us too.'

'Let me talk to her.'

Eddie commented to his wife, 'Perry is not a criminal. He was jailed for giving shelter to a fugitive. That boy Paul is not a criminal. He was in jail for six months for a petty crime. He can't handle sudden wealth. He lacks the guts to be a criminal.'

That evening Paul was arrested for the alleged murder of Ronald Parker. Eddie was shocked to receive a call from Paul seeking help. He called his Probation officer to suggest a good lawyer and arrange to represent Paul in the case. He suggested Ruth Crawford, 'If she can't get him acquitted, no one can.'

Eddie was confused but, believed that his own assessment of Paul was right.

He had seen criminals in jail and outside. Paul doesn't have it in him to murder anybody.

He remembered Paul's last words before he bid good bye to Eddie.

'I was in prison for six months. I am not going back.'

Eddie sighed sadly.

RUTH CRAWFORD

Ruth Crawford was not happy. She is a successful criminal lawyer. Professionally, she has no competition. Whenever she accepts a case, the prosecution gets fidgety. She is capable of creating sensations in defence of her clients. She says that she is a lawyer and defends her clients with commitment. She says that it is for the judge to convict or set the accused free. She, therefore, works with a clear conscience. Her husband Henry Johnson, a partner in a stock broking firm had been cheating on her. He has been spending a lot of time with Grace Kelly. Due to her contacts with the police, prosecutors, detectives and other lawyers; she was getting information about the affair with proof of his physical relationship with Grace. There were CDs, particulars of the hotels frequented by them. She had unassailable evidence to support her in a divorce suit. She took the CDs but did not bother to see the contents as she trusted Henry. She realised that she had been complacent while her marriage was breaking up. They had been married fifteen years. She is forty years old now. They have no children. They were not in a hurry. A few weeks back, Grace called and invited her to dinner at a restaurant. Ruth accepted. During dinner, Grace confided that she and Henry were spending time together and had been sleeping together frequently for the last eight months.

'I am not claiming that I am a superior woman. These things happen. I do not wish to intrude into your family life, but Henry had assured me that your marriage had been on the rocks for a long time. I don't want to spring a surprise on you. I know that it is difficult to reconcile to the fact that he is leaving you for my sake'

Ruth said 'I am hurt and feel insulted. My husband is leaving me for another woman. I thought that our marriage was a success. I am glad that you met me and explained the situation. Divorce will be very expensive for Henry. He may not have much left. Would it be alright, if I discuss this meeting with Henry ?'

'Ok. He should know that I do not want a secret relationship with him. If he is not prepared to accept me publicly, I do not want this relationship. I am pleased that I have taken the initiative and met you. Thanks for listening to me patiently and sympathetically.'

'I appreciate your concern for me. In a situation like this, it is rare that the third person in the relationship comes forward and tries to sort out the situation. It is nice to meet you.'

'I hope that I haven't hurt you. I felt that you should know what is going on. Here is my mobile number. We shall keep in touch. I repeat that I do not fancy myself superior to you because Henry is leaving you for me, love is blind.'

'I thought love doesn't wear off. I am disappointed that Henry doesn't love me anymore. This is a disaster. I am not happy but I have to face the situation and come to terms with whatever is happening. Henry doesn't get off lightly. He is going to get the Archimedes' screw.'

Grace laughed and asked, 'What is that.'

'It is a shaft with a blade 4 to 6 inches wide that spirals around the shaft. It will lift water from lower source to the higher level. I am angry and used it as it came to my mind. I meant that he will get difficult time from me.'

'I will leave now, bye.'

'Bye.'

It was a Saturday, time was 5:15 PM, Mrs. Richard, Lady Katherine and Ruth were sitting in the garden of Sir Robert's. There was a round table with biscuits, cakes, etc., laid there on. They were meeting for tea at the instance of Ruth. Normally there are five or six ladies who meet once in a month and spend time together. This was an emergency. Lady Kate and Mrs. Richard were all ears for Ruth's narration.

Ruth said, 'I confronted Henry with the info the next morning. He treated the matter as frivolous. He said "Grace was an accident. There is nothing serious between us. I slept with her only once. I told her not to take it seriously as I am married to an exceptional woman and that I am in love with her." I was shocked at his nonchalance.'

She stopped to cry. Mrs. Richard hugged Ruth and said, 'Don't cry my child. You are an extraordinary woman. You have the courage to face this situation. It takes time to recover from a soured relationship.'

Ruth continued, 'When I told her Henry's reaction, Grace took it lightly and said that it was instant reaction as he was surprised at the confrontation. She was rationalising that everything he had been doing was to get closer to her. That woman was soaking in the fantasy of love. I felt that it was more than I can stand. I showed Henry, the door. I asked him to leave my house. He tried to plead that he loved me and said that I was making a big mistake. When I did not relent he packed his belongings and moved into Grace's house. I am devastated. I am not able to reconcile to the events and am crying when I am alone. The whole world can see my shock and anguish. I am not smiling any more. I do not understand the logic behind his effort to explain his conduct. He had already taken the decision to leave me.'

Lady Kat said, 'God's gift to mankind is forgetfulness and adaptability to the situations. You will forget the humiliation and the agony and return to normal. People like Henry deserve to be forgotten. Get the thoughts and memories of him out of your mind. Start living normally.'

The butler entered garden and a signalled to Lady Kat. Lady Kat went to him, listened to what he had to say and returned. After a few seconds Siva walked up to the table and greeted Mrs. Richard with great pleasure. She was moved by his reaction.

'Siva, it is lovely to meet you again.'

Lady Kat introduced Siva to Ruth, 'Ruth, this is Siva. He has come from India to study the space sciences. He did his engineering in India and possesses software skills. Siva this is Ruth, a barrister. Siva has been living with us for the last two weeks, and is leaving us now as he feels that he is not earning his pay.'

'It is a pleasure to meet you Lady.' he said to Ruth.

Ruth replied 'I am not a lady. I mean you do not call me a Lady. That is only for Lady Kat.'

Siva turned towards Lady Kat and said 'Good bye, Lady. Thanks for everything. I shall keep in touch with you.'

He nodded to Mrs Richard and Ruth and left.

The butler escorted Siva to the door and the waiting cab. He said, 'Good bye, Siva. I am sure that we will miss you.' He smiled.

Sally met him two days later and asked, 'Why did you leave Sir Robert. They are disappointed.'

'I do not have enough work to deserve my boarding and lodging. I felt that I was living like a parasite.'

'You saved him from a dangerous situation.'

'That is over. People like him should not keep their Email accounts dormant. They should check their accounts periodically and change their passwords. Lucky that we discovered that somebody hacked his password and were logging into Organ Bank in his name'

'You can go back whenever you want.'

'Sir Robert gave me that option. When I went to the ladies to bid good bye, I found that the atmosphere at the table was gloomy.'

'It is on account of Ruth. Her husband left her for another woman. She was heartbroken and is unable to reconcile to the situation. She was not attending the court for the last seven days. People accused of serious crimes are depending on her as she is their counsel.'

'She is a criminal lawyer?'

'Yes, she wants you to develop some project, which is about legal matters.'

'I think I can handle that project. I cannot handle Sir Robert's work. I have no knowledge of his subject of work and research. When does she want to talk to me.'

'Today, if it suits you? We can meet her at 6.00pm today.'

'We ? Are you coming with me.'

'Yes, be ready by 5.30 pm.'

Ruth greeted them pleasantly. Siva was impressed with the ready smile from the people in UK, US and Europe despite serious domestic and health problems. Except for the sacks below her eyes, nobody can detect the shock and grief that engulfed her.

After the introduction, she said, 'Siva, I need you to programme a software that is time consuming. We will feed the data available from the cases I am dealing with. We will also feed the laws of evidence. After we enter the data of the prevailing Laws, the software should highlight the clinching evidence that will determine the fate of the defendant.'

'That can be done. But, nobody can predict how the judge will interpret the law and the evidence.'

'What do you mean? Judges analyse the evidence and decide if there is any violation of the Law. They give clear guide lines to the jury before they rise for their deliberations. Some judgements become laws. We will decide on the judgement after the software throws up a solution.'

'When do we start?'

'Tomorrow, if it is convenient to you.'

'That is alright with me.'

'I have two cases which are under trial. We shall start with them. One is young boy of 20 yrs accused of murder. I believe he is innocent. But the circumstantial evidence against him is over whelming. The other is a Mexican accused of smuggling a kidney, heart and narcotics into London. An organ bank is reported to have ordered them. The indent from the organ bank and invoice from Panama are forged. I hope to get an acquittal at the time of preliminary filing of charge sheets.'

Sally said, 'Siva discovered that Sir Robert's password was hacked to log in to the organ bank's website. Siva alerted Sir Robert and the police.'

'Lucky, that the hack was discovered. Otherwise, after two or three transactions, Sir Robert would be accused of organ trafficking and lose his reputation and be tried.'

Ruth said, 'It is nice to meet you, Siva. I will give you the records of both the cases. Feed the data into the PC. I will give you the laws of evidences too. You can feed the information into the PC. Take your time. The case of Paul Blake is in advanced stage. Take it up first. The case against Carlos Gonsalves is yet to come up for trial. They will file the charge sheet in a day or two.'

'That is alright, I will commence the work tomorrow. Where would you like me to work. At your chamber in the court or at your home ?'

'Work here. I will give you the key to this house. You can enter the house even if I am delayed and not yet come home. You can raid the fridge, drink some tea or coffee and help yourself to the cookies and pastries. You can make yourself comfortable. I live alone.'

'I can deduce that you are single for only a few days from the puffiness under your eyes. It is none of my business, but I pray that you get the courage and strength to tackle whatever is bothering you.'

'Thank you. You may as well know. My husband left me for another woman. May be I did not pay attention to him as I was busy with my legal practice. I should have noticed the change in his attitude to our marriage.'

'The most widely quoted and used advice from the Geeta may give you some peace. It is, "You have only the right to action and not to the fruits there of." You act as the situation and circumstances demand. The fruits of your action are decided by Him. You do what is required to be done and leave the consequences to Him. There is no alternative.'

'Thank you, I think that you gave me the answer to my predicament. I will milk my husband dry. I will set the process in motion and let it run on its own course.'

While driving back Sally said, 'You have the knack of making people like you. They answer your prying questions which would annoy people.'

Siva read the case history of Paul Blake's trial. He was convinced that he was guilty of murder. He appeared to be regular visitor to the murdered man. On 6th October, the omnipresent CCTV cameras of London had caught him entering the house at 9:30 am. He prepared breakfast for himself and the murdered man. He left his fingerprints everywhere. He spent a lot of time in the house. He had taken the shower and took breakfast to the murder victim. He could have killed the man, but Ruth says that Paul found the victim's body and left the house in a hurry. The CCTV camera caught him leaving the house. He was agitated before leaving the house. He called emergency number and reported the murder. The voice matched with Paul's. The motive for the crime was the dispute in sharing some loot.'

He was still at work, when Ruth returned. She was surprised and said, 'There is no hurry for the project. You are young, decent and handsome.

Girls will be interested in you. You can get a date. Don't spend your life working in the nights.'

'Alright, I will leave in few minutes. There is a discrepancy in Paul's case. The victim died five hours after post–mortem.'

Ruth laughed, 'The victim must have died on the 5th October. The prosecution must have filed a correction memo.'

'The defendant's deposition was his whereabouts on the 6th'.

'It may not make any difference. He is an isolated case. He has the skill of building up evidence against himself.'

Next morning she visited Paul and whispered, 'Where were you on the evening of the 5th October.'

Paul said, 'What does it matter. I was set up and framed in this murder. I am innocent.'

'But your whereabouts on the 5th October are important. Your friend must have died on 5th. Paul's face lighted up in a flash and became sullen.'

'Call me to the witness box and ask me the question. I am afraid of giving the information prematurely.'

'I am your attorney. I am here to help you.'

'I know. Please call me to testify again. You will like the answer.'

'I cannot accept that. I should know what I am getting in to. If you don't trust me, get another lawyer. As it is, there is overwhelming evidence against you. You left your finger prints all over the place. You admitted to taking the cash from the cupboard which belonged to the victim.'

'He wanted me to take it,'

'We have only your word. There is no corroboration.'

'He executed a Will leaving all his property to his brother living in Canada. He left the cash on hand to me.'

'Where is the Will?'

'I don't know.'

'How much was the cash on hand?'

'About 7,000 pounds.'

'Did you depose so in your examination?'

'Some of It. You did not attend the court last week. I was not asked the right questions. The attorney's name is Albert.'

'He is the senior most of my juniors. He is good. Well, I must say good bye. Find another counsel.'

'Please, don't leave me. I will give you the information. The murder victim participates in intraday trading in the Stock Exchange and is successful. He works on two jobs and makes a lot of money.'

'Where were you on the evening of the 5th October?'

He whispered something into his inter com. She got the sentence clearly. Her eyes sparkled for a second.

She said quite seriously, 'Don't even smile during the trail. You are not out of trouble yet. The evidence you possess can be presented to the court by an Advocate.'

That evening, she told Siva, 'Tomorrow is my lucky day. I am going to go for the prosecution's jugular and get acquittals for Paul and Carlos.'

'With this kind of optimism you will forget your grief about your marriage. It is good riddance. That man does not deserve a wife like you.'

'You are flattering me.'

'No. I speak the truth. You are a successful lawyer, good looking and have the strength and competence to face the present situation.'

'You sound convincing, but I cried in Sir Robert's house.'

'That was the first reaction.'

'You are speaking wisely. Will you come to dinner with me?'

'That will be a privilege.'

'Wait for me, I will freshen up and come'.

She took a shower dressed in casuals. Siva stared at her.

'Let's go.'

She felt better.

Over dinner, Siva commented 'Why did Henry deny his relationship with Grace. He must have planned to surprise you. You pre-empted him and in surprise must have tried to make light of it.'

'Let's not talk about him. That will spoil the mood. I am happy now. How could Sir Robert allow you to leave?'

'I wanted to leave. He paid well. The perquisites were free board and lodge. I was not doing him any service in return. He has no project. He has enough IT support personnel in his office. I felt guilty taking his money.'

'You discovered that his pass word was hacked and saved him from trouble with the Law, even though the Court finds him not guilty after prolonged trial.'

'That was over. There is nothing more to do.'

Siva stood staring at her, 'I revise my comment about you being good looking. That is an understatement, you are beautiful. I pity the man who left you. He does not deserve a wife like you. It is a good riddance.'

She was enjoying the conversation. She needed reassurance and that is what Siva is giving.

'Thank you, let's go.'

'Sir Robert lives like a Lord. He is highly successful in his research, business and maintains the family's estate. He maintains a large house hold and lives like the nobles of the empire in its golden era. But, I wanted to leave. He paid me well. The perquisites were free board and lodge. In return I was doing nothing. He has no project. He has enough I.T. support personnel in his office. I felt guilty taking his money.'

'You found that his password was hacked and somebody accessed into the Organ Bank's web site by logging in his name.'

'That was over, there is nothing more to do. I was adequately compensated by his employment for two weeks.'

After dinner, they returned to her house. She said, 'Thank you, for the evening. I enjoyed it, I am returning to normal. Tomorrow will be my day and I am going to win.'

She gave him light hug and kissed him on the cheek. He grabbed her into his hands and hugged her strongly. She could not resist him and yielded to him.

After half an hour, she got up, poured herself a drink and looked at him. She was not angry, though she was shocked. 'What have you done? I can sue you for rape. There was no provocation for your action.'

'You did not resist. I could not control myself.'

'I admit that I did not resist. I wanted to but could not. You are in danger of being accused of rape. Do not do such things in future. You are not fired. Return to work as usual.'

'Good Night.'

After overcoming the initial surprise, she realised the she felt at peace. That boy is divine. But she cannot have a relationship with him. He will get into trouble if he reacts like he did with innocent and good natured girls have their hands around his neck and touch their cheeks to his cheek. She did not care about the divorce now. She will instruct her solicitors to go for a settlement that will milk him dry. She is now ready to get on with her work. When she attended the court the next day, her colleagues in the court greeted her affectionately. The judge also greeted her with a broad smile and said, 'We missed you, Ruth'.

'Thank you, your honour'

The prosecution of Paul Blake commenced. The prosecution called Mr Arulmugam Viswanatha Pillai. Mr. Pillai walked along the gang way, entered the well of court and climbed into the witness box. He was duly sworn in.

The prosecutor asked him, 'What is your business?'

'I am a partner of Pillai and Menon, the firm of solicitors.

'Do you know the deceased?'

'Yes, Ronald Parker was our client. We prepared the will executed by Mr. Parker'.

'What are the provisions?'

'Mr. Parker bequeathed his entire property to his brother living in Canada.'

'Anything more ?'

'Yes sir, he bequeathed the cash in the chocolate box in his ward robe to Mr. Blake, the accused.'

'Did you find the chocolate box?'

'Yes.'

'What did it contain?'

'It was empty?'

'Did you make any effort to find out what happened to the contents?'

'We learned that Mr. Blake had taken it.'

'That is all your honour.'

Judge looked at Ruth, 'Counsel for defence may examine the witness.'

Ruth walked up to the witness box and asked, 'Mr. Pillai, What would you have done if you found the cash in the chocolate box?'

'We would have counted it and handed it over to Mr. Blake against his receipt.'

'Did Mr. Parker explain his reasons for bequeathing the cash to the defendant?'

'Mr. Parker expressed very high regard for Paul Blake. He stipulated that Mr. Blake was free to take the cash when he finds it and that we should take the receipt for the amount admitted by him and discharge him.'

'Did he give any reasons for leaving the cash for the Blake?'

'He considered Mr. Blake a victim of circumstances and that he was Mr. Parker's handy man. He felt that Mr. Paul Blake should be helped for rehabilitation. And that he was working in that direction.'

'Was all this recorded in the will?'

'Yes, if you want, I will read the content aloud.'

'That is not necessary, that is all your honour.'

The Judge looked at the prosecution.

'No further questions, your honour.'

Ruth stood up and said, "Your honour, the defence would like to question Dr. Martin, the forensic surgeon.'

The Prosecutor jumped up and said, 'Objection your honour. Dr. Martin was examined and the cross examination was done by the senior defence counsel. Recalling the witness when the trial is over and arguments are about to commence is unnecessary. Recalling Dr. Martin is an attempt to drag the trial in search of some sensation or technicality. Dr. Martin has to be served the summons. It may take a day or two.'

'Delay of one or two days is not going to hurt the prosecution. A man's life is at stake?'

'What do you expect to prove,' asked the Judge

'There is a discrepancy in the date of death.'

'Yes, the prosecution has filed a correction memo and was accepted by the court. You were not present in the court.'

'The typing error was committed by Dr. Martin. The correction memo was signed by the Prosecution. If Dr. Martin committed the error, he should correct it in a fresh deposition. I want to find out whether the error was regarding the date of death or the date of report?'

'Overruled. Let's recall Dr. Martin.'

'Your honour, I have taken the liberty of requesting Dr. Martin to be present in the court today. There he is.'

'Dr. Martin, take your place in the witness box.'

'He was questioned and cross examined and discharged. He should take oath again.'

The prosecutor made a gesture of exasperation. The Judge looked at him and said, 'Does it hurt if he swears again?'

'The prosecution will examine him first.'

'Please go ahead.'

'Dr. Martin, how long have you been doing post mortem operations.'

'Objection, Your honour.'

'What is it about?'

'The prosecution is not getting to the point and is establishing the witness's credentials. We have accepted his expertise and integrity. Error can be committed. To err is human.'

Yet, the prosecutor was harassed. He said, 'The post-mortem reports are in a standard format. After reading them over the years, we tend to jump the format and read only the cause and time of death. An error in the date is unfortunately over looked by us.'

'You are apologetic about the error that can wait, let Dr. Martin depose.'

'Dr. Martin, when did you receive the body for the post-mortem?'

'At 11.05 am on the 6th October. That was recorded correctly in my report. The cause of death was a massive blow to the back of his head with a blunt object such as a baseball bat, cricket bat or the butt of a gun. The time of death was estimated to be between 7 to 9 pm on the previous day, which is the 5th October, when I was typing the report, I erroneously recorded the date of death as 6th October instead of 5th October. Such errors are committed very rarely. This was the first time.'

'Can there be any error regarding the time of the death?'

'No, Sir. I have provided for any adjustment when I put the time of death between 7 to 9 pm on 5th October. I will stake my reputation on the time of death.'

'That will not be necessary, sir. That is all Your Honour.'

The Judge looked at Ruth and said, 'Your witness, Mrs Ruth.'

'No questions your honour.'

The Judge looked at her and said, 'You recalled him.'

'That is right your honour. The prosecution has established the date and time of death. We have nothing to add. My next witness is Paul Blake, the defendant.'

'Objection, Your Honour. She is conducting the trial again.'

Ruth replied, 'The prosecution has not recorded the where abouts of the defendant between 7 to 9 pm on the 5th October.'

'Overruled. The defendant shall take his place in the witness box.'

'The Prosecution wants to question first, your honour.'

'No objection your honour, the defendant should swear again.'

The Prosecutor asked the defendant 'Do you remember where you were between 5pm to 11pm on the 5th October 2012.'

'Yes sir.'

'Will you please enlighten us where you were at the time?' asked the Prosecutor with sarcasm.

'I was in the custody of the Twickenham Police from 11Am on 5th OCT to 9.30 am on 6th Oct.'

There was a soft murmur in the court hall.

The Judge said, 'The court is adjourned for fifteen minutes to enable the Prosecution to verify the defendant's claim.'

When the court resumed, the Prosecutor declared that the defendant was right. The Judge dismissed the case against Paul Blake as the prosecution failed to prove his guilt and released the Jury.

He looked at the prosecution and said, 'You are the Prosecutor in the case of Queen Vs Carlos Gonsalves.'

'Yes, Your honour.'

'Can we take it up today?'

The Prosecutor discussed with the police and said, 'We can produce the accused after lunch.'

'Is the defence counsel ready?'

'Yes, Your Honour,' replied Ruth

'Then, the court will reassemble at 02.00 pm today'

When the court resumed after lunch, the accused was presented to the court. The judge looked at the accused at length. He was impressed with the bearing and the body language. He also felt that the defendant was confident of the acquittal.

The bailiff asked the accused to stand up. The Judge asked Carlos, 'You are indicted on two counts. The first charge is that you trafficked human organs with fake documents,. Do you plead guilty or not guilty?'

'Guilty, Your Honour.'

The Judge expected him to plead not guilty. The prosecutor and the police hugged each other with pleasure. The Judge looked at them sternly with disapproval.

He asked the accused, 'The second charge is that you have smuggled 10 kg of heroin or cocaine into U.K. Do you plead guilty or not guilty?'

'Not guilty, Your Honour.'

'We shall commence the trial of the second charge.'

Ruth stood up and addressed the court, 'Your honour, I request the court to give me five minutes to explain the charge.'

'You will get abundant opportunity during the trial and arguments.'

'I beg Your Honour, not to admit the charge, it has no basis.'

'That is alright. You will get your time during the trial.'

'No, your honour, the charge is frivolous, unwarranted and waste of the court's time.'

The Judge looked at her with impatience, but, ruled 'I am surprised that you have very low opinion of the Prosecution. Permitting you to speak now is like starting dinner with dessert. Your representation better be good. Your request is allowed.'

'Thank you, Your Honour. The Prosecution has no case. The Police did not find any narcotic substance in the possession of the accused or in the luggage or the container of the human organs. They have no evidence except a presumption.'

The judge looked at the prosecutor and asked, 'Is it true?'

'Your honour, I have been representing Her Majesty the Queen for the last ten years. I was never accused of filing a charge sheet without evidence. We shall prove that the accused is guilty.'

'The only evidence is not even circumstantial. It is based on an assumption.'

The Prosecutor stood up and said, 'Objection, your honour.'

'Sustained. Please go ahead with the trail.'

'Your Honour,' intervened Ruth; 'Let the prosecution describe their evidence and how they propose to prove the case. If they have a single shred of evidence, we will plead guilty.'

Carlos was alarmed. But he did not know what to do. His Attorney is picking a quarrel with the Judge.

'The Court has experienced your skills of getting acquittals on technical grounds. You are also prone to theatrics, and sensationalise the issues, to destroy or twist the evidence. But, what you are asking the Court is unusual. The Court has observed your career with respect and admiration. The Court will allow your request. If the court finds that you have arguments based on frivolous reason, it shall treat that your behaviour is in contempt of the Court and deal with it accordingly.'

'Objection, Your Honour.'

'What is it now? You are objecting to my observation.'

'I have lot of respect for the British Law and the Judiciary. Neither the Jury nor the Judge will be influenced by my theatrics. All the decisions taken by the Courts were strictly according to Law. The Courts should be convinced beyond shadow of reasonable doubt that the defendant is guilty. They take serious view of the cases of physical assault. I humbly submit that your comments about my methods of handling the trials influence the Jury and the Judge are uncalled for and not true. We are all proud of the fairness and the highest standards of our Judiciary. The Court is in contempt of itself.'

'Sustained. The Prosecution shall give a brief gist of their evidence.'

'I congratulate the defence attorney. She gets away with those comments. She is good looking and intelligent. She uses her faculties shrewdly and wins her cases.'

'The Court finds that your comments that the Judge and the Jury are influenced by her beauty and the brain are uncalled for and irrelevant.. The court takes umbrage at your insinuation that those attributes influence the Judiciary are in contempt. The Court is lenient with you, this time. I am sure that you are merely admiring her and did not mean any contempt of the Court. Go ahead with the brief summary of your evidence. The prosecution shall explain their case in short as abundant opportunity will be available during the trial. The counsel for defence pleads that the charge is not maintainable and should not be admitted.'

The Prosecutor lost his composure. 'Your honour,' he croaked, 'The accused brought genuine human organs with false documents. The human organs were transported in a metal container which is similar to the water dispenser. While leaving the airport, he went to the customs and declared his cargo. After the customs cleared him, he waited for an hour for somebody to come and take over the merchandise. He then used the aero bridge to check into the hotel. There was a difference of 10 kg in the weight of the container at the customs and weight after confiscating the container by the narcotics agency.'

'Your honour,' Ruth intervened, 'the accused was closely followed from the customs department to the hotel. He was out of sight only for five minutes. When the investigating agencies broke into his room, they found him taking a shower. The investigating agencies gave him some rope in the hope of capturing his contact at the airport. They rushed into his room immediately after he checked in and he had no time to remove the 10kgs of narcotics.'

The Judge asked the prosecution, 'Is that right?'

'Yes, Your Honour, there is no logic behind transporting human organs with fake documents and declare it to the customs dept. The circumstantial evidence is over whelming.'

'There is no direct evidence. The havoc that can be caused by the circumstantial evidence is seen by us in the case of Paul Blake,' commented Ruth.

The Judge ordered, 'Mr. Prosecutor the Court will adjourn for five minutes during which you can decide whether to press charges or not. After that, the court shall rule that the charge is inadmissible.'

After the adjournment, 'The Prosecution has decided to drop the charge. The charge may be treated as withdrawn.'

The Prosecutor sat down and whispered to the lawyers sitting next to him, 'On any other day, with any other defence counsel, we could get a conviction on the evidence available even though it is flimsy, from the same Judge.'

The other lawyer commented, 'The broad is beautiful, persuasive and convincing. It is difficult to resist that combination. Ruth is ruthless.'

The Judge said, 'As the accused pleaded guilty, it is only the quantum of sentence to be determined. The Jury is discharged with apology.'

The Prosecutor stood up and said, 'We ask for maximum sentence which in this case is 12 years.'

'That is heavy. Can you substantiate?'

'He was involved in trafficking human organs. There is no shadow of doubt regarding his involvement in the trafficking of human organs. He broke the law wilfully.'

'Has the defence anything to say?'

'Your Honour, the defence submits that the accused may be released with censure.'

'That is frivolous. He was guilty.'

'He pleaded guilty to transporting the human organs. He was not aware that he would be breaking the law. He is a victim of a wicked plot by a crime syndicate. All the documents were prima facie in order. It is beyond his means to discover that the documents were false. Both the procurer and receiver were respected organisations. He would have passed through the customs, had it not been found that the password of a prominent member of the organ bank was hacked.'

'But, he broke the law, Your Honour. He may have done it in good faith, but he broke the law of land. The Law is that transporting or trafficking of human organs is a crime. There is no exemption to transporting them wilfully or innocently, in good faith without his knowledge that he was committing a crime.'

'The accused is 22 years old. He has no history of crime. He was gainfully employed and his employer is happy with the services of accused. By sending him to prison we create a criminal. The British Law is not cruel. The Judge has discretion. There are several instances of the Judges who used their discretion.'

'You may have a point there.'

'Your Honour, the defence counsel is mocking the law of our country.'

'She is doing her duty.'

Ruth pressed her advantage, the Judge apparently agreed with her.

'Your Honour, you may sentence the accused to some period on probation, it needs a work permit. He may have to stay in this country. He may eventually settle down here.'

'If he is sent to prison, Your Honour, that contingency does not arise,' suggested the Prosecutor.

'The prosecution has a valid point.'

The Prosecutor beamed with pleasure.

The Judge pronounced, 'The accused in this case has pleaded guilty to the charge of trafficking human organs in violation of the law of this country. He is therefore, convicted of this crime and is sentenced to one and half years in prison and a fine of 1,000/- pounds or another six months in prison in lieu thereof.'

There was jubilation and hugging from the prosecution benches. The judge banged his hammer on the table and shouted "silence" with anger and impatience.

'In view of his young age, decent and crime free history and he being the victim of a crime syndicate's plot, the court takes lenient view and has decided to suspend the sentence. The accused may be set free.'

Ruth smiled broadly. Her face beamed with radiance.

The Judge said, 'Will the counsel for defence stand up?'

'Yes, your honour.'

'The law has provided for punishment for contempt of court, but there is no provision for distracting the Judge with the good looks, radiant smile and lot of intelligence. The court is defenceless. As the Court's business is concluded, the court adjourns and reassembles as usual tomorrow.'

Ruth was on cloud nine, this is her day. The acquittals and the Judge's complements had an electrifying effect. She was not standing on the floor. Her body was three inches above the ground.

The prosecutor jumped to his feet and said 'Objection, Your Honour.'

'What is it? I vacated the bench and am in the well with Lawyers.'

'You are claiming monopoly of your feelings towards the counsel Ruth.'

'Yes.'

'The Prosecution and the lawyers sitting next to me have the same feelings towards Ruth.'

'Sustained. I expressed my own feelings. I am delighted that everybody feels the same way.' He shook her hands and retired to his chamber.

On the way home, she bought a bottle of champagne and some Italian food. She called Siva and asked him to be at her house by 7 p.m. She told him to cancel any other engagements he may have. Siva told her that he was free. She can take all the complements and flattery, but Siva can express his feelings better.

When Siva arrived, she told him, 'I had an excellent day at the court today. Paul Blake and Carlos Gonsalves were acquitted.'

'Congratulations. I am happy that Carlos is acquitted. You told me that he was to plead guilty to the first charge. In that case, he would be sentenced for a term in prison.'

'Yes. He was sentenced to prison for one and half years and a fine of 1000 pounds. I talked the Judge into suspending his sentence and free Carlos.'

The calling bell rang when she opened the door, she saw Carlos, Margarita and Paul Blake happily grinning.

She said, 'Come in. Normally I expect my clients to contact me at my chambers in the court. Please settle the bills there.'

'We brought a bottle of champagne for you. We thank you for everything you have done for us. You were wonderful in the court. Please do not open the bottle. We have planned our celebrations at our hotel. We know that we cannot barge into your house unannounced and impose on you. We came here to thank you and give the bottle of champagne. We will leave now.'

Margarita asked, 'What does the "suspension of a sentence" mean?'

'It means that he is free for the present. If he is convicted of any crime in future, he serves this sentence too. The evidence regarding the trafficking is direct. There is no point in contesting the charge. That was the reason why we pleaded guilty.'

They left leaving Ruth and Siva, 'I am not in a mood to receive people to my house today.'

She opened and poured the champagne into two glasses and gave him one.

Siva said, 'I never drank liquor. This is the first time.' and took a large gulp.

'I cannot resist you. You are beautiful. Your husband is a dumb ass. He left you and it is his loss. Can I spend the night with you.'

'O.K. You have to leave early in the morning.'

'I will. Thank you.'

'Let me be frank. I cannot have a relationship with you. I cannot get you out of my mind. I don't think I love you. I have to resist the thoughts of you. I have, therefore, dropped my project and you are fired. In case you need anything, please let me know. We will not meet again. I am guilty of exploiting you to overcome the trauma.'

'I am surprised and humiliated by your reaction. I have not taken advantage of your situation. I will leave now.'

'I am now free of worries. I don't care for my husband and his friend. I am at peace. Now, I have to sort out my priorities and organise my life. You are a distraction. You have done me great service and I am grateful. Please do not take offence at my behaviour.'

RONALD PARKER

Ronald Parker graduated in economics. He was 24 when he completed his graduation. He went steady with his high school friend. After a courtship of one year, he married Dorothy. Their marriage lasted for four years. They broke up and have divorced after a mutually agreed settlement.

He did not remarry. After his marriage, he got a job in the finance department of an oil company and was posted to Kuwait. Kuwait was rebuilding after liberation from Iraq. After serving for four years in the oil company, he quit the job to join a firm of stock brokers. That firm trades in shares, derivatives and options in all the major stock exchanges. He was exposed to the capital markets. But, things did not work out in his marital affairs. Dorothy wanted to return to London. Ron could not adjust to the discord in the marriage. After Dorothy left, he devoted his time to the stock analysis and understand the principles and practices of trading in the stock markets. He stayed in Kuwait for another four years and returned to London. He was thirty two years old.

A day after landing in London, he went in search of his ex-wife. She had married again and has a daughter. He did not make any effort to contact her. He left his visiting card under the door of her house. He did not receive any response from her. He decided to try and forget her.

During his eight years in Kuwait, he earned and saved considerable amount. He was single and needed to spend very little for his day to day affairs. He used that money to trade in stock exchanges. With his experience he was earning profits.

One evening, he strolled out of his house for sun. He came across a Lebanese restaurant.

When the waiter approached him to take his order, Ron said in Arabic 'I want some coffee.' Two men sitting on the adjacent table turned their heads and looked at him sharply.

After three days, they called on Ron at his house and sought some time. One of them said, 'My name is General and this is Admiral. We are name less and identity less. We work for an intelligence agency of the British government.'

Ron asked, 'MI5 or MI6?'

'Neither. We are a separate entity reporting to Ministry of Home Affairs.'

'What can I do for you.'

'We want you to join us. We will pay well, we avoid leaving clues to our office, but the pay will be made in cash.'

'What do you want me to do?'

'We want you to snoop on the telephone conversations, chatting in internet, E-mails etc., of a given identity. You listen to the activities of the people using that medium and translate and drop your report in a drop box for us to collect.'

'You will be paid 7000/- pounds pm. All you have to do is sit at home and keep your eyes and ears open,' said the man called Admiral.

'Sounds easy, I will not do the field work and attack or kill people, I will not break the law. Since snooping on the conversation of some Arabs on behalf of the Government is in the interest of national security, I don't mind doing it.'

'Good, we will send you a P.C. with the required software. Someone will come and install the system.'

'Tell your man to ring me before setting out to my house.'

'He will.'

'We will give you the number of a cell phone. Call that number in case of emergencies only. Within a minute of your call they will trace the locations of both the phones and our cover will be blown and our lives will be in danger. The Arabs we are snooping are tech savvy. That is the reason why we use the drop box instead of the electronic medium.'

'What kind of emergencies are you talking about?'

'Threat to your life, the intercepted dialogue may be about a terror attempt. Use your discretion.'

'O.K, It is a deal?'

'Expect to receive the necessary equipment in a few days. You will also receive the training to use the software and snooping and logging in to the other computers and hacking.'

'That is wonderful.'

Ron met Paul Blake at Eddie's Breakfast. He saw Paul coming out from the office door behind the counters and collect a plate full of breakfast without paying for it. He saw Paul settle down at a table. He was interested in the boy. He was hardly twenty years old. He carried his tray to the table where Paul was sitting and asked, 'May I sit here.'

Paul nodded. Ron observed that the boy was casting furtive glances around. Ron sensed that he was not welcome. After moving over to that table, Ron had no choice.

He concentrated on his breakfast. He asked curiosly, 'Do you work here?'

'No, I do odd jobs for Eddie. We are friends, I am not an employee. Eddie is a friend.'

'Will you do odd jobs for me too?'

'Yes.'

'The work will not be difficult or heavy. Come to my place in the evening. What is your name?'

'Paul Blake.'

Ron was sitting on the couch and was reflecting on the events of his life. After divorcing his wife, he had not met another woman. Time used to run very fast in Kuwait. As a trader in the stock broking firm, he was either trading for the firm or analysing the listed companies' shares with the information available. He was assisted by the analyses of the firm. He was aware that the share markets are not influenced by the economic fundamentals, but by sentiment. He never ignored the fundamentals.

After moving to London, he started feeling lonely. He is yet to meet a girl to go steady and think about commitment. He preferred not to take up a job, but trade for himself.

He was doing reasonably well. Paul Blake arrived at his house and rang the bell.

Ron opened the door and asked Paul to come in. The Intelligence installed the snooping equipment and bugged a telephone and e-mail account and the house. There was recording equipment which would enable Ron to follow the activities of the users of the telephone and e-mail and the house. Ron would commence his work right away. The recording machine is switched on. He would snoop live and record it too. He learned that Paul's parents broke up when he was twelve. His mother got the custody. She brought him up as best as she could. When she remarried, his step father treated him affectionately. But things were not the same. Both the parents were struggling to make a decent living. Paul dropped out of school and lost direction. He saw no purpose in life. At nineteen, he was caught shoplifting and was sentenced to eight months in prison. After three months, he was granted parole and was released. The Probation officer recommended Paul to Eddie. Eddie already met him. He did not mention that he knows Paul. Paul too did not let on.

Eddie knows Paul to be an honest and sincere person. There is no streak of criminal in him. He assured the Probation officer that he will take care of Paul. Paul vowed to never go back to prison.

Ron told him, 'Your work with me is quite simple. I will give you an envelope every evening. You should drop the envelope at the address given. That is all. You will get five quid for each drop. The drop changes periodically.' Paul found, this work convenient. He spent his free time with Eddie and Ron. He spent more time with Ron as there was no pressure of business. He enjoyed complete freedom with Ron. The fridge was at his disposal. Ron kept some money in a drawer in the ward robe and told Paul was welcome to take it if he needed money. But, It was left untouched during the three months Paul had known Ron. Around 11 am on Thursday, the sleuths of Twickenham police arrested him for stealing from a super market. They read his rights. Paul did not know any lawyer. He rang up Eddie. Eddie could not leave his work. He rang Paul's Probation officer. Meanwhile the police interrogated him during that day and were convinced that he had nothing to do with the crime.

After keeping him in custody for the night, they released him at 9.30 am on Friday. As Paul did not turn up that evening Ron went out for a walk and dropped the envelope. He had dinner in a restaurant and returned home.

He sat in front of his P.C. and was scanning through the shares he traded that day. He suddenly jerked with pain and died. He did not feel the second blow. He did not know what hit him.

At 9.45 am on Friday Paul knocked on the door of Ron's house. The door was not locked, he opened the door and entered the house and shut the door behind him. He went straight into the kitchen helped himself to breakfast. After that he went in to the bed room to see if Ron was awake and needed his breakfast. Ron was not there, he went to his work room and found that Ron was dead, lying in a pool of blood. He was scared. He had to leave that place immediately. He checked the drawer of the PC used for trading in shares, there was a small roll of currency held together by a rubber band. He went to Ron's bed room. He opened the chocolate box and took the cash. He needed the money. Ron gave him the permission to take the cash on hand. He went into the living room. There was Ron's mobile phone. He used it to call the emergency and reported that a murder had been committed and the dead body was lying in a pool of blood. He gave address and disconnected the phone. He left the place in a hurry. He left his finger prints all over the place. Two days later, he was arrested on suspicion of murdering Ron Parker. When he was allowed one phone call, he called Eddie and sought his help. Eddie promised to arrange for a lawyer to represent him. The Probation officer rang up the police and contacted Paul and advised him to co –operate with the police.

The police were questioning him about his whereabouts on the 6th. He knew he was being framed. When his lawyer came to talk to him, he was surprised to see a beautiful and soft spoken woman. He told her that he was being framed. He did not commit the murder.

'I am innocent. Ron was kind of my god father. Even though we had been friends for only four months, our friendship had become strong.'

The lawyer introduced herself as Ruth Crawford, said, 'Why did you take the 232 pounds in the drawer?'

Ron asked me to take the cash in the drawer whenever I needed money and also the money in the ward robe.'

'That is only your word, there is no corroboration. I am convinced that you are guilty as hell.'

'Won't you represent me.'

'I will. I am not the kind of attorney who only accepts cases that are likely to be won. There is the Judiciary. I don't judge people. An accused person is entitled to explain his position and defend himself. You have no alibi. The circumstantial evidence is overwhelming.'

'I have really no reason to kill him. In fact, his death is a blow to me.'

'They did not find the murder weapon. They could not establish a motive for the murder. Another computer with recording equipment is destroyed and no clues are available in that angle. You called the emergency number and reported the crime, but you did not reveal your name and your identity. The Police have a strong case against you. It is so strong that they are celebrating your conviction before the trial commenced.'

'I was set up. I was a petty thief. I do not have whatever it takes to murder a man.'

'That is what everybody says. We will fight the charge to the best of our abilities. Pray for some luck.'

DONALD PRICE

Donald Price is twenty four years old. He is 6'2" in height. He is slim and handsome. He is Sally's boyfriend. His father is chief of a Shipping Agency and owns it. Donald helps his dad in his office. His dad pays him a lot more than any other employee with similar responsibilities. He is of cheerful disposition. Sally and Don were drinking coffee in Starbucks in Staines one evening. She saw Siva and Mary enter and squealed with pleasure. She waved her hand to draw their attention and signalled to them to join them.

When they came to her table she asked, 'Will you join us. If you want to be alone, we will meet some other day.'

Mary looked at Siva for a moment and said, 'We will join you. We can spend some time together'

Sally introduced, 'Don, this is Siva I told you about. Siva this is Don Price. Mary, this is Don, this is Mary a deputy detective of London Metropolitan Police.'

After shaking hands, they took their seats. Don asked 'Mary, you must have exciting time in your work.'

'Yes, I was fascinated by the police. I wanted to be a mounted police. When I wrote the test I knew that I would pass. I wanted to ask for the mounted police wing. But they selectors have allotted me to homicide and other crime.'

'You solve murder?'

'Criminal investigation is a matter of collecting evidence and persuading the witnesses to testify. Solving murder like Sherlock Homes is not possible these days. The Judges will not accept the deduction. They want hard, direct evidence. Confessions to crime at the police station are not accepted.'

'That must be difficult.'

'Yes. It is difficult, but that is the job. Dying declaration in the presence of a judicial officer is being shred and invalidated as evidence by sharp counsels for the defence. I am not complaining. I like my work.'

'That is good. Siva, how do you like friends in Metropolitan Police?'

'I am awe struck by the police. They have a reputation of being friendly, sharp and efficient. I enjoy the company of Mary. She doesn't talk about her work.'

'You are interested in space technology. It must be tough studying that subject.'

'I like it. I am interested in the subject. That makes the subject interesting to study.'

'It is nice to meet you and Mary. I work for my dad in the family business.'

'Your study of space sciences and Mary's job in the Police are challenging. My work is so ordinary.'

Siva replied, 'I was fascinated with the sky since I was three years old. In summer my parents used to sleep in the open terrace. My mother used to sing lullabies about the moon and the stars. We used to gaze at the sky and the stars. Space technology is basically robotics and remote control.'

'What do you plan to do after passing out from the University?'

'I want to work for two or three years in the organizations in U. K. or NASA in U.S.A. or ISRO, the Indian Space Research Organization in India. After that I propose to set up an industry for manufacturing components required by agencies engaged in space research. That industry will also manufacture Robots both Industrial and domestic.'

'That may require a lot of capital.'

'Yes. The Indian Banks and the government will support high tech projects. If they are not convinced about the viability of the project, I will opt for raising the capital through market and public issue of shares.'

'Things may not work out as planned. I am not throwing cold water on your aspirations, but be prepared for unforeseen hurdles. Best of Luck.'

After fifteen minutes, Siva and Mary left the restaurant in search of some privacy.

Don commented 'They are interesting couple. But, they cannot get into serious dating as Mary will not leave her job and Siva has plans to return to India.'

'They are not a couple. They are only friends. They are aware that a commitment for long term is not feasible,' replied Sally and continued, 'When Siva speaks about the sky, you cannot but admire his passion for space.'

When Don dropped her at her home, he kissed her passionately before saying "Bye."

Sally walked in to her room with a heavy heart. He told Sally that he is averse to sex until the marriage. She appreciated his principle. They have been dating for the last four years. He did not make any attempt to make love to her nor did he propose.'

After seeing Siva and Mary, Don felt that he had been amiss in treating Sally. He was not interested in other girls and had been true to her. Most of the boys have girlfriends, Don is different. But she found it impossible to maintain. Girls are anxious to lose their virginity. She felt that there is more than principle in his behaviour. When she met Siva the next evening in the High Street, she spent some time with him.

Sally asked him, 'Am I plain or lack the charm to attract men.'

'When I told you that you were beautiful, you snubbed me. You told me that I was dark and therefore could not hope to make love to you.'

'Forget that conversation. I am asking you now.'

'You are beautiful and rich. These two qualities make you the most eligible bride. I like you and will make love to you given the opportunity.'

'Thank you. Don't get any ideas. It will not happen. You are dark and there is cultural incompatibility.'

'The cultural incompatibility is to be considered when we are contemplating marriage. We can have sex without taking it seriously.'

She laughed, 'You have graduated from flattery to propositioning. I am not interested.'

'Keep in mind. I am available whenever you are ready.'

'I want you to give your opinion about Don. We have been dating for the last four years. He had been very decent. He never wanted to make love to me. All my friends slept with their boyfriends. The boy friends keep on suggesting sex. Don had been different.'

'May be he is not a hetero sexual. He is perhaps queer.'

'If he is, he should have told me. I have waited years for his proposal. It did not come.'

'You suggest it.'

'It hurts my ego, I will not beg him.'

'In that case, I will talk to him.'

'Don't do anything. It is none of your business.'

'I don't think he will wait any longer. This has gone on for too many years.'

Next evening when they met, she asked Don, 'When am I going to listen to the words from you?'

'What words,' he asked, 'Oh that. I have learned only a few days ago. The company of a beautiful girl was not exciting. I have the crush on your friend Siva, I realised that I am gay. I am sorry. I love you, but that does not make any difference.'

'Well, you told me now. That is a big relief. Siva is not gay.'

They finished their dinner and got up to leave. She declined his offer to drop her at her home. When her daughter entered her home her mom noticed the frustration and anger in her daughter's face.

She asked, 'What is the problem, honey, you appear to be unhappy.'

'It is Don, mom.'

'Did he hurt you or had been rude to you.'

'No. He had been very courteous. He told me that he realised that he was gay.'

'Why didn't he tell you all these years?'

'He learned that he was gay when he got the crush on Siva.'

'Is he gay too?'

'No, He is normal. From the first sight, he has been trying to get me to sleep with him.'

'Don is a decent boy. I would have approved if he proposed. Siva is different. He is outstanding in his education and has a direction in his life. You cannot but fantasize with him when he talks about space, stars, galaxies and space travel.'

'He speaks to you?'

'Yes, I asked him to come by whenever he is free.'

'Mom, you are trying to manipulate me.'

'Don't be alarmed. It was only for tea and small talk. He said yesterday that the planet Venus is under greenhouse effect. The atmosphere of Venus is lined with a layer of carbon dioxide which reflects hot air from the planet back to it, thereby increasing the heat further. The atmosphere in Venus is heavy and not accessible.'

'Yes, Space is his passion. He is always talking about the speed barriers and the ways of overcoming them. He has great dreams.'

'What is the speed barrier?'

'It is the speed of light which is approximately 186,000 miles per second. If you travel at that speed it will take more than 600 years to reach a planet that could have atmosphere similar to earth.'

'He did not tell me. He told me that all the planets in our solar system spin on their axes toward east except Venus. Sun rises in the East. Venus spins on its axis towards west in exactly opposite direction. He explains that it turned upside down some time during the last billion or more years ago.'

'That is fantastic. He is a light in the tunnel.'

'I am disappointed that you misunderstood my equation with Siva. Don't think that I am nudging, but you will be very lucky if you marry him. He is divine.'

'Mom, I am hungry.'

The butler arrived and announced that dinner was ready.

Two days later, Frank Miller approached her and asked her, 'Will you have dinner with me tonight. I hope you are free.'

'I am free, but I don't know if I am ready for a date now.'

'You are disappointed with Don. I know about Don. That is disgusting after all those years.'

'I do not want to talk about Don. He is handsome, sportsman and making a comfortable living.'

'Don has been postponing the reality. He was averse to accept that he was gay. With a girlfriend like you he did not have the courage to accept his sexual preference. When he realised that he could not put it off any longer, he told you and lost your friendship. He has been silently suffering since he declared that he was gay.'

'He does not lose my friendship. He cannot marry me, that is all.'

'He was hoping that like some men, he could enjoy gay sex and sex with women.'

'Thank you for your concern. You have not spoken ill of Don. You have been fair in explaining his predicament. But, I am not yet ready to date another man. Please give me some time.'

'Take your time. If you decide not to accept me, I will be disappointed.'

After a few days of persuasion Sally accepted an invitation for dinner with Frank. She really enjoyed his company and his cheerfulness. He works in a Bank in a middle management capacity. He has a promising career. His job is secure. People in his pay grade don't leave the organisation, but work till the retirement is due. True to his career, he talks about finance, shares and derivatives. Frank is ambitious. He has no patience to work for 35 to 40 years in a Bank.

Even though Frank never expressed his unhappiness with the Banking career, she sensed it. She is still interested in Don. She meets him frequently. He was kind, considerate and makes you feel important. She regretted that she could not marry him. Frank is interested in money. Most of the time she spent with him, he would discuss money. She felt inadequate in his presence.

'Mom, Frank is very impressive. He is confident of earning millions of pounds and control a multi business empire. But, I do not love him. I miss Don.'

'What is the point in loving a gay? I still think that he is a very decent boy. I will be delighted if you married him.'

'I have an Indian girl in my class doing her MBA in Finance. She has many interesting things to discuss.'

'I will be glad to meet her. Why don't you invite Siva and her to "At Home" in our house next Saturday? Sir Robert, Kat and Ruth will also attend.'

'That is great.'

'Frank, Siva, Sally, Ruth and Sir Robert and his wife attended on Saturday. Frank and Sundari were introduced to the gathering.

Siva explained, 'Sundari means beautiful woman.'

Everybody clapped. During the conversations, Sir Robert commented, 'With the increase of base rate, the interest on housing loans has gone up to 6.5 % p.a. and more. That is a big blow to borrowers.'

'That is soft,' said Siva, 'Interest @6.5 % p.a. is soft. In India, the minimum interest rate is 8 % which is applicable to borrowers with very good credit rating.'

Frank commented, 'Interest at 6.5 % p.a. is usurious. Imagine the burden on subprime loans.' Sundari intervened, 'Interest at 6.5 % p.a. is cheap compared to Indian conditions. Low interest rate is a characteristic of high consumption economy.'

'What do you mean?' asked Frank.

'Countries in Western Europe, U.K., U.S. and perhaps Canada are high consumption economies. The characteristics of high consumption economies are low interest rate, low inflation and availability of credit in abundance. As these are free market economies, the competition is heavy. The profit margins are narrow. The profits are achieved with high turnover. Therefore, consumption is encouraged. Credit is available at soft rates.'

'I never looked at our economy in that perspective,' said Frank.

Sundari continued, 'You have the provision of fore closure of loans. The Banks, worried about the financial health of its borrowers can fore close the loan. That demolishes the borrower as his means of repayment of loan is closed. There is no provision of fore closure in India.'

Ruth commented, 'Sundari, you have good grasp of Finance. You explained our economy in simple language.'

'Thank you.'

Frank was impressed. This girl is not merely talking about Finance. She summarised the macro economics with ease.

Ruth said, 'Sir Robert, the courier who brought a kidney and heart to deliver to your Organ Bank is now free.'

'That poor man was a victim of criminal manipulation. I am glad that he was acquitted.'

'No, he was not acquitted. He pleaded guilty to the charge of trafficking human organs. He cannot deny that. He pleaded for lenience.'

'If he is not acquitted, how come he is free?'

'The judge sentenced him to one and half years in prison, but suspended this sentence and set him free.'

'What happens to the suspended sentence?'

'If he is found guilty of crime in future the suspended sentence will be enforced in addition to the latest sentence.'

FRANK MILLER

During lunch break, he told his boss, 'Yesterday I met some interesting people. There was a girl from India doing her MBA in London with Finance as her option. She has opinion on the current crisis. She says that we are a high consumption economy where interest is low to encourage consumption.'

'Working in a Bank, we tend to react to things as they come. We are in a rut. Somebody like that girl gets a bird eye view and notices things we fail to see. She must have commented about the subprime loans.'

'She did. The banking sector flushed with low cost funds has identified a new market in the housing loans for subprime borrowers with disastrous consequences. The Banks and the financial institutions were of the opinion that the loans to borrowers with bad credit history are secured by the primary security of the house purchased with the loan. They did not imagine the collapse of market for real estate with so many properties coming up for sale or auction. The concept was applauded as a brilliant idea. Now they blame the Banks. The critics say that the pay and bonus packages for the executives are undeserved.'

'Did she have any suggestion to overcome the crisis?'

'Yes. The failure of the subprime loans has affected the liquidity of the Banks and financial companies. They were unable to match the increased bad debts with any increase in their liabilities. They could not take possession of the assets and sell them in large numbers, leading to crash of the real estate market. It had caused a chain reaction and the economy has gone into recession. When the purchasing power of the people is affected, raising the base rate of interest worsened the situation. The markets are revived if the people buy. Therefore, she says it is appropriate if the base rate is reduced.'

'That was done. Ask her if she is interested to join us. We can always use that kind of talent.'

'I will.'

Frank was fascinated with that girl. He asked her to dinner a couple of occasions. He had seen her a few times with Siva. He asked Siva if he was interested in her.

'We are both from the same place. Our mother tongue is Telugu. So we are close. There is no talk of marriage or love.' replied Siva.

Frank tried to kiss her at the door when he dropped her at her home. She politely pushed him away. She lives as a tenant in a single bedroom.

The land lady asked her, 'Why don't you kiss him. If you are not interested, you can kiss him on the cheeks and thank him. You are driving away the boys.'

'I am yet to break the cultural barrier.'

The land lady treats Sundari with affection. She wakes her up with bed tea and serves her breakfast. She cooks her dinner and charges her reasonably. She spends some time talking to her and enjoys her company.

'You can ask him to come inside. I can fix him a drink, alcoholic or hot beverage. You must pay for it though. Next time when Frank dropped her at her house, she asked him to come in.

'This is a surprise. I am pleased that you asked me in for a drink.'

She said, 'I enjoyed your company. Most of the local boys want to have sex and suggest it by gestures or by expression of interest but the situation with the girls is different. If they are in a relationship or a wed lock, they stay true to it. They don't talk to strangers. The maximum concession allowed is a smile, when the eyes meet. Colleagues, classmates and the like are accepted and they talk to them. But strictly no intimacy. Men are different. They proposition to you as soon as possible.'

'Where do I fit in this set up?'

'You are a friend, not a boyfriend. I cannot have any relationship with you as I return to India in another eight months.'

'I can fix you up a job in our Bank. It will be a career. You don't have to go back.'

'I am engaged to a man in India. My fiancé is waiting for me eagerly. I want to marry him.'

'Well, I am disappointed, but that is life. You have done me a great favour by not allowing the relationship to develop.'

'I am sorry to say no to you. You are handsome, decent and have a good and secure job. I don't understand why the girls are not after you. You are capable of taking care of a woman. You can give a girl security and love. The Lucky girl is waiting for you out there, you will find her soon. You are my friend and we can continue to see each other.'

'Thank you. Your opinion on this subject is comprehensive. I will take leave now. I will meet you again. You have the ability to explain complicated situations in simple manner. Bye.'

'Bye.'

DIANA WOOD

Sundari, Frank, Siva and Sally were sitting in a restaurant in the high street in Egham.

Frank asked Sundari, 'You commented that the low interest rate is a characteristic of high consumption economy. If that is the case, why did the competent authorities raise the base rate?'

The countries are facing the balance of payments crisis. Most of the Banks' funds are deployed in the subprime loans which have become Non Performing Assets. The mounting bad debts have affected the liquidity of Banks and financial Institutions. They had to provide for their mounting bad debts. Their equity is eroded. They were seeking bail out from their governments. Alan Green span raised the U.S. bond rates by 25 basic points consecutively seven or eight times. Increase of 50 basic points in bond rates used to attract institutional investors, who with draw their funds in countries like Mexico and India, for example. The investments of these funds in stock exchanges were withdrawn and were deployed in the U.S. treasury bonds. Countries that have used these funds to finance their balance of payments short fall suffered calamity in money supply. The Reserve Bank of India realised that the funds coming into the stock exchanges are volatile and left them untouched. So, India did not suffer from the funds crunch to meet its B.O.P. Bank of England raised the base rate at least eight times consecutively. The RBI did the same, but that is not working now a days. The stock markets in the developing countries are yielding more returns.'

Siva said, 'You are well informed in economics and share markets.'

'I have done project assignments as a part of my curriculum. I collected data. I think I am arrogant to discuss the impact of the monetary policies of Central Banks. I am quite sure that I am wrong.'

'What is wrong with analysing and drawing conclusions.'

'The people who manage these central banks are highly qualified and experienced in managing the economies of their respective countries. People like me comment on their policy decisions. I don't have their expertise and access to the data and information they have.'

'There is nothing wrong with that.'

Paul Blake walked in and greeted Siva.

Sally asked, 'You know him?'

'Yes, I work part time at Eddie's Restaurant. He too works there.'

'He is a convicted criminal. He was tried for the murder of a man.'

'He was acquitted. One small crime of stealing from a super market had landed him in prison. He learned his lesson. He is desperately trying to make an honest living. But the shadow of criminal record is making his life difficult. Eddie is helping him.'

'Sigmund Freud said that the person who committed a crime once, would do it again.'

'Paul Blake wouldn't.'

'Are you sure? He tried to steal from a super market. He murdered a man for small amount of cash. The prosecution attributed a small amount of cash as the motive for the murder.'

'No. The deceased left a Will. In it he bequeathed the cash on hand at his residence to Paul. The solicitors were instructed to accept Paul's word regarding the amount taken by him'.

'If he is so reliable, why did he commit the crime.'

'He mixed up with a few people prone to crime. His father died when he was two years old. His mother raised him for four years and she remarried. The step father treated him well. But he could not raise the child after his mother's death. Thereafter, he grew up in an orphanage. He did not know the father's love. He remembers his mother's love and considers the years he spent with his mother as the golden age of his life.'

Frank intervened, 'Talking of love, I have a few questions. What is love? How do we recognise it? What if one loves a person and the person does not reciprocate?'

Sundari replied, 'You are asking questions that were debated for centuries.'

Diana Wood walked in to the restaurant. She recognised the group. Frank, Siva and Sundari looked at her appreciatively. Diana noticed their attention and was pleased.

Sundari said, 'Now that you have asked the questions, let us try to answer them. Everybody should give their opinion.'

Siva opened the discussion to say, 'The question of love comes openly in the case of marriages. You have no choice regarding your parents. The love of mother is god send. It is a divine blessing.'

'So if we define love, we can also set the parameters for the selections of the spouse.'

'Let's first understand love. While the mother's love is permanent, the child grows more and more independent and by the age of 14 to 19, the baby leaves the home in search of livelihood or a trade or a skill.'

His sexual urges make him go in search of suitable partner for life. The grown up baby is attracted by a person of opposite sex. If the baby is concerned about the needs of the would-be partner and longs for the company of the new partner, the person would be sexually attractive. He sees a spouse in her. But marriage is more than love or sex.'

'1. The love should be spontaneous.'

2. It should be as strong as the mother's love which can be treated as affection and concern for the wellbeing of the grown up child and

3. The intended partner should be sexually desirable.

With these qualities the friendship leads to marriage and the journey to the adventures of life.'

'Sundari, you have not considered the financial aspect,' said Frank.

'That is important for some and some don't care. It is very important. It will have a great impact on the marriage. Poor people marry too and live happily. We are only looking at the human angle. While the mother's love is permanent, the love between married couples is subject to wear and tear.'

Siva said, 'This is a storm in the tea cup. We have discussed love and marriage. But such cold blooded analysis is not love. Love should happen.'

'There is nothing wrong in trying to know whether you love a person and how.'

'Ultimately we can conclude that the marriages are made in heaven.'

Frank said, 'I know a person who behaves as Sundari described. I am not going to name the person for some time.'

Paul reappeared and went straight to Diana and sat across her. Siva and Sally looked at them curiously. They wondered about the connection between Diana and Paul. Diana got up from her chair and approached the group. She smiled and said, 'I have over heard your discussion and want to join. Can I join you ?'

Sally said, 'Please take a chair. I know you. I have seen you at Sir Robert's house.'

'I am his assistant. I am doing my research in Bio-technology. Sir Robert is my guide.'

Sally introduced the other members of the group.

Siva said, 'We have completed our discussion and we are about to leave. Shall we order tea for you?'

'No, thank you. We can meet some other time. I have to pay my bill. It will take five minutes. Sir Robert spoke very highly of you. Next time you visit Sir Robert give me a ring. I will join you.'

'Alright,' he took her card.

Paul was making signs to Siva to talk to him. Sally noticed and told Siva, 'Paul wants to talk to you desperately.'

Siva walked up to Paul. Paul whispered, 'Give me a five pound or ten pound note. I don't need the money. Diana Wood wants to talk to you. Find some time after the group breaks up and when you are alone, give me a ring. Matter is urgent.'

Siva gave him ten pounds and returned to the group.

'Paul had a drink and found that he does not have the money. Luckily, I am available.'

Sally offered to drop him at his place. Diana said that she would drop him as she was going that way.

In Diana's car Siva asked, 'What can I do for you.'

'I will tell you. Let us pick up Paul, who will be waiting at the gas station nearby.'

She stopped the car at the Wait Rose parking lot and said, 'I am the owner of the house where Ron Parker was murdered. I was present in the court during the trial. I met Paul a few days after his release. I found a couple of pen drives. I cannot make head or tail of it, will you help me decipher the context. Paul tells me that you are highly skilled in the software and hardware.'

'That is an exaggeration. I am trained, but not experienced. As the character in the movie, "From Russia with love", said, "Training is useful, but there is nothing to beat the experience."'

She laughed. She drove to the house. The three of them entered the house. She took them to the room where the computers are located. It is a small house semidetached. There is some open place in the front and the back. The computers are located in the room that over- looks the green back yard. She picked up the two pen drives and handed them over to Siva.

'As he was working when he was killed the computers were not shut down.'

Paul said, 'The place used to be full of pen drives. He was "burning" the data in to the pen drive. The pen drive was sent to his employers and the copy stored in the hard disk.'

'The killers checked both the computers. The computer used for his trading in stock exchanges was left untouched. They removed the hard disk of the other computer and took it away.'

'How do you know there are more than one,' asked Siva.

Diana spoke before Paul could answer, 'There must be two people, one man to kill Parker and another to clean up the memory of the recording computer. They replaced the hard disk with another containing movies and porn.'

Siva said, 'The police thought that the crime was solved with the arrest and prosecution of Paul. Even if they did not suspect Paul, they would not have got any suspicion as no info was available from the second computer.'

'Paul, do you know what he did with second computer?'

'No, I do not know.'

'Diana, you have to inform the police.'

'Yes, I know. I am afraid for my life.'

'We should not have come to this place.'

'Yes. Police handed over the keys only yesterday.'

'They have kept this crime as unsolved until further information is available. They are ignorant of the activities in the second computer.'

'I will call Mary and inform her.'

He dialled Mary's number and when Mary answered, he said, 'Mary, this is Siva.'

'I know, your number is in my phone book.'

'You remember the case of Ron Parker's murder?'

'Yes, we have given up our investigation. We are waiting for further developments. What is it about?'

'We have some more information in the case.'

'Very Good. That will do me some good. Where are you? I will come and collect the new evidence.'

'We are in Parker's house, please don't come here. We may draw unwanted attention. We will meet at our usual place at the Starbucks in Staines High Street in half- an –hour. We will bring the evidence with us.'

'O.K. You are removing the evidence from the scene of crime. Please take photographs of the position and location of the evidence taken from all the eight angles.'

'All right.'

When the trio entered the Starbucks, they found Archibald and Mary sipping coffee. They waved their hands and invited the trio to join them. Any bystander watching this scene will believe that the meeting was accidental.

Archibald asked, 'What is this about. We are holding our breath in anticipation of sensational information.'

Siva said, 'Diana found two pen drives in the house. That means Parker was not sick sexually. I have not seen the contents of the pen drives, but they change the direction of the investigation.'

'Do you have the pen drives?'

'Diana has them. We have not seen the contents.'

'Copy the contents to another pen drive and place the original pen drives exactly where you found them.'

'We have not removed those pen drives.'

'We copied them into the laptop of Siva.'

'What is in them?'

'I don't know. They are like conversations. There is written matter too.'

'What do you make of it?'

'I think Ron was snooping. The conversation is in foreign language. Most possibly it is Arabic. It could be Urdu too.'

'There are Arab numerals. It is most likely to be a telephone call.'

'Perhaps we stumbled on a terrorist cell.'

'That is the most likely answer.'

'Mary, we will go and collect the evidence. We were carried away by the circumstantial evidence and booked Paul. If there was a clue like this the investigation would have gone in another direction and we would have lost jurisdiction over the case.'

Mary said, 'That is possible even now.'

Archibald said, 'Siva you go home verify the contents and give us a clue. Meet Mary at 8'o clock and take her to dinner. That is your date with Mary. The date is sponsored by London Metropolitan Police.'

Diana said, 'People will love the police if they arrange suitable dates.'

There was loud laughter at the table before they dispersed.

Siva said, 'I have gone through the matter in my laptop. There were a lot of telephone calls. They were recorded. Voices were converted to text and their translations were written in English. Parker was given only one number to snoop. That was in the shadow. One is most likely to overlook it. He was copying all the records to a pen drive and sending the pen drive to somebody.'

'That takes the case out of our jurisdiction. That is O.K. Was the language Arabic?'

'Yes, they must have discovered the snoop, traced it to Parker and killed him.'

'That was a professional job. Whoever did it is used to kill people. It is difficult to trace. "Impossible" is the word'

They spent an hour or so together. Siva dropped Di at her house and went home.

Exactly one hour later, the police raided Parker's house and recovered the pen drives. During dinner, Siva explained to Mary, it is impossible for a man like Paul to inflict such blows to Parker. Paul has neither the courage to kill nor the ability to inflict such injury.'

'You cannot rely on that, for we do not know the ways of death. People have died following a slip on the steps. I have heard of cases where people have died after a mild tap to the nose.'

'You could be right. Recently, I read about the murder of Trotsky in Mexico.'

'What is that about?'

'Trotsky was a communist who escaped to Mexico to avoid Stalin's purges. He was living in exile. But, Stalin did not want to leave loose ends. He sent a 25 year old KGB operative to kill him. He went to Trotsky's house to hand over a letter from a Russian dissident. Trotsky was eighty years old. He had sparse hair on his head, which was parted in the middle.

While he was reading the letter, the young man removed a pick axe from the inside of his long coat and hit Trotsky on the parted line. The axe did not penetrate the skull, but rebounded. Trotsky screamed in pain and grappled with the killer. During the struggle, the man pulled out a gun and shot him, seconds after Trotsky's wife ran into the room. Trotsky was no match to 25 year old KGB agent. He was killed while his wife watched helplessly.'

'So, what does it say?'

'Under normal circumstances the axe with a stainless steel handle of one foot would have penetrated the skull. Trotsky took the blow and yet grappled with the assassin. This proves that the ways of death are difficult to understand.'

'So, you say that it was within his means to kill Parker?'

'Certainly not. Paul doesn't carry weapons. He did not have whatever it takes to murder.'

Mary said, 'Remember the conditions of this date?'

'What conditions?'

'Archibald only arranged the date. He is not financing it. We don't need him for the date. We have been dating without his help.'

'Please come to the point.'

'You have seen the contents of the pen drives. We should discuss the contents of those hard discs and see if there are any grounds for police action.'

'Parker was listening to the phone calls made and received by the phone under surveillance. In fact the entire house was bugged. The telephone calls were informative. They do not seem to have used a mobile. All the calls were to the land line. Parker was recording the voices and giving a translation. Most of the conversations were trivial. They were in Arabic. In order not to confuse with other numbers, the telephone number was indicated on top of the recording in a shadow. Here is the telephone number.'

'Did you get the meaning of the conversations?'

'No. They were trivial matters, but there must be a code. It appears to be the controlling centre for terror operations.'

'Do we have the telephone numbers of the others?'

'Yes, they are available.'

'Good. Let us order dinner and drinks.'

'I am going to delete the contents of those pen drives when I go home.'

'Wait for my word. Let us take a look whether the contents are clear and readable. I will call and tell you.'

After dinner, he dropped her at her home and returned to his house. There was a text from Mary which read "O.K".

Siva deleted the matter from his laptop and went to sleep.

Archibald and Mary met Siva at the coffee shop.

Archibald said, 'Siva, you have the gift of getting into situations with law. Not on the wrong side of course.'

Mary said, 'We raided thirteen houses simultaneously, but we were late. We wasted a lot of time trying to get Paul convicted.'

Archibald said, 'The birds have flown. We reached a dead end.'

Mary said, 'The case relates to an international terror group. A counter terrorism wing of a British intelligence organization must be tracking them. There is nothing we can do now. We are closing the case as unsolved for the present.'

Frank walked in and smiled at Siva. Siva invited him and introduced Mary and Archibald. He told Archibald, 'Frank works in a Bank. He is a career Banker. He can be consulted about Stock markets. Futures and derivatives trading is also part of his activity.'

Mary asked, 'Banks are reported to be in trouble now.'

'If the Banks are in trouble the economy is in trouble. Present state of the economy is on account of Banks and the financial institutions.'

'When do we see the good days?'

'The Banks and financial institutions need a bail out from the government. But the economies will recover sooner than expected.'

FRANK MILLER

Frank Miller had been friends with Sally since their school. They dated frequently and were going steady until Donald Price arrived. Things changed drastically. He lost Sally to Don. Sally was interested in Don and Frank gradually retreated after he realised that Sally was in love with Don. He suspected Don was gay. He had the best of everything he could ask for. He is friends with a heiress to millions of pounds. His girlfriend was truly in love with him. Don refused to face the symptoms. He put it off for unusually long time. First he discussed with his mother. She did not show any sympathy.

She said, 'Don, I am disappointed with you. I am biased against gay sex. I am old fashioned and traditional. I am proud of it. You have the world at your feet and you are gay. I don't think that you are gay. But if you are, there is nothing I can do. Don't expect me to attend your gay wedding.'

Don didn't get the help and support he expected from his mother. He knew that his father would be more strongly against gay activities.

Finally, he informed Sally. Sally was devastated. She still loves him but in a platonic way. There is no way she can marry a gay person. Sally is still concerned about the welfare of Don. Frank Miller had taken Sally out about three to four times, but withdrew when he realised that she was not in love with him.

Frank's father told him one day, 'What is wrong with you? You are handsome, educated and have decent job in a Bank. You are not likely to leave this job. The job is secure and there are opportunities for promotions. Find your girl, there is someone waiting out there.'

His mother said, 'You should take the girls out to dinner. Don't miss the chances out there. From your description, I understand that you are mixing up with a police woman and a research scholar. Both are good propositions, "Best of luck".

Next day, he rang up Diana and invited her to dinner. She agreed to meet him. Diana had little time to pursue personal relationships. Yet, she felt that the invitation by Frank was exciting and irresistible. They had good dinner and talked passionately about their work. Time flew.

Sally suggested "at home", periodically, say once in a fortnight like their elders. This was accepted by everybody. They drew lots and Siva's turn came first. They agreed to meet on the next Saturday. Siva called Sally and asked her if it would be proper to hold "at home" in a restaurant. My place is not suitable. The "at home" will be outside the home.'

Sally laughed and said, 'Let the first tea party be at my home. The next meeting will be at Frank's place or Diana's house. The three of us will make arrangements on rotation basis. The group consisted of Sally, Siva, Sundari, Frank, Diana and Mary. Mary's attendance was subject to the pressure of work.

The common topic was about marriages. All of them were single except Sundari who is single but the marriage is few months away. The topics of conversation depended on whatever came up.

Sundari raised the topic of marriage. 'I observe that both boys and girls in the western culture go through lot of struggle and pain in selecting their spouses.'

'That is the only way. The decision cannot be imposed by anybody. Even friendly or affectionate advice is rejected,' said Mary.

'The youngsters are expected to fend for themselves. They should be assisted by the well meaning elders. Some people may require help. They may not be capable of finding a suitable life partner.'

'In that case, they may end up as spinsters or its opposite number.'

'Mary, that is what I am trying to say, love is three kinds, first it is love at first sight, second by long association and third by mutual need. If the boy and girl have been together for a long time, they develop some affinity. This is common in Indian marriages. Love by mutual need is difficult to explain. A divorcee with custody of children needs the comfort, security and support of marriage. A person in similar situation will be looking for a spouse. I think, the second kind is sustainable. I feel that love is not permanent and is subject to wear and tear,' said Sundari.

Frank said, 'Sundari, you have opinion on every subject.'

'I take it as a complement even though it sounds cynical.'

'You have an answer to the current economic situation?'

'When a subject comes to my notice, I read about it, analyse and try to understand it. I could be wrong.'

Mary asked incredulously, 'Do you have an opinion on the current economy?

'I do, but, I have the humility to admit that I am in no way comparable to the persons controlling and monitoring the economies of their countries. The Governor of Reserve Bank of India is more qualified and experienced in his field. The Governor of RBI, is usually a Ph.D., in economics or its allied subject, or has handled responsible positions in the world bodies monitoring the global economy and assisting the countries in need. You do not become a Governor of RBI, if your thesis for Ph.D. is about the marriage rituals of the Bentus. The current Governor of the Reserve Bank Of India had warned the developed countries that the western economies are heading for the current situation four years ago.'

Diana said, 'We are deviating from the point. We were discussing love.'

Sally said, 'When you love some body, you may realise it later, after missing the opportunity. Love sometimes goes unnoticed. When you are happy and peaceful in the company of a person, then you can recognise that feeling is love.'

'Diana, you have some opinion on love?' asked Frank.

'No, I thought about love, but gave up the effort as I was not getting anywhere. I agree with Sundari's analysis.'

'What is your activity?'

'I have a post graduate degree in Bio- technology. I am continuing my study through research. I am interested in Eco-protection.'

'Saving the earth from environmental disaster is the top priority,' said Mary.

Sundari commented, 'That is a priority today. Did anyone consider the influence of culture on environment?'

Diana said 'I understand your question. By 13th century A.D. India had made several advances in science. The Indian and Chinese cultures were more advanced in science and in the protection of environment while the western states were still in dark ages.'

Sundari said, 'The first blow to environment was agriculture. It led to deforestation. The western model of development was a disaster for environment. Any new discovery was transferred to class room in the next academic year. The new technology was transferred to markets within one year. The consequences of technology on environment was realised only after the damage was done.'

Sally said, 'The development model was user friendly. The science and technology were used to make people live in comfort and happiness. May be this is the only way.'

'We can only imagine the eastern model of development,' said Sundari.

Diana commented, 'The western model of development created uncontrollable debris. There is debris in the sea. The garbage debris of towns and cities is somehow manageable but the effect on environment was big. Then there is the nuclear debris. The debris in the space is becoming hazardous.'

Frank said, 'Hearing you talk about science and technology makes me feel like a nonentity. I feel that I am so ordinary.'

Sally replied, 'What about me? I do not understand the stock markets. You have exposure to stock exchanges, hedge funds, futures and so on. I have studied English for my graduation. I do not have a trade or special skills.'

Siva listened attentively. When they broke up he commented, 'Frank, today's "at home" was quite interesting. That girl Sally is capable of loving.'

'She still cares for Don. Pity, he had to give up Sally. They are still good friends.'

'I admire Sundari. She can make conversations on tough subjects quite simple.'

Siva asked, 'You are going steady with Mary. Best of Luck to you.'

'Mary is an adventure. Her job is exciting and revealing.'

'What does she reveal?'

'The dangerous under world. When she talks about her work, you are thrilled.'

'I met her in an unusual situation. When she realised that I am not a criminal, she took interest in me. Spending time with her was a pleasure.'

'I am thinking of proposing to her.'

'Do it, She deserves a man like you.'

A few days later, he proposed to her and she accepted. The proposal was a happenstance. It came out abruptly during conversation.'

He had taken her to meet his parents. They were happy and relieved. They welcomed her warmly to their family. His mother was doting on her and causing embarrassment.

His mother said, 'Mary, you are an angel. Frank is lucky. You will have a happy marital life. There is always the third degree to control him.'

Frank's dad chuckled. The family dinner was sumptuous and tasty.

Mary said, 'Frank, your parents were delighted with me and excited about your marriage.'

'They were worried about me. I never took a girl to meet them. They were disappointed that I was not doing what I should at my age.'

'Really? I am surprised. You are the most eligible bachelor. Why didn't you get along with girls?'

'I was interested in Sally. We have been together since our school days. Proposing to her was a mere formality. Then came Don. She fell in love with him. I did not stand a chance.'

'We will announce our engagement at the next "At home."'

'O.K., Meanwhile I will buy a ring for our engagement.'

Mary was driving the car. She was in the high street and took a turn towards Staines. Suddenly they heard loud and short sounds. Mary became a police woman. She picked up her mobile and rang Archibald, 'Gun shots were fired near Egham bus terminal. Proceeding to the crime scene. Rush back up with ambulance.'

Frank was white with fear. 'Mary, why do you want to go to the crime area. They were gun shots fired to kill. You put your life in danger.'

Mary did not say a word. She drove the car at great speed. She was not driving a police car. There was no siren and no Police Network phone in the car. When they reached the area, they saw a man lying dead in a pool of blood. They saw a silhouette of a man in the darkness. Mary pulled her car to a stop, pulled a service revolver from the glove compartment and jumped out of the car.

Frank groaned, 'Mary, what are you doing? That man is killer. You are in danger.' She did not hear those words or ignored him.

She pointed her revolver at the man and said, 'Drop the gun and raise your hands.'

'You think you are a cop? Take this,' he said and fired at her. Mary said, 'Frank, get out of the car and crawl to safety. Crawl away from the man. Don't hesitate. Your life is in danger.'

'What about you?'

'Don't worry about me. Get going.'

'You got your boyfriend? I will give him a taste of lead.' and fired at him. Frank dropped to the floor before the man fired and escaped the bullet.

Mary was repeating her demand. 'I am warning you, drop the gun and raise your hands or I'll shoot.'

'Why don't you come here, we can have sex. Don't act like a cop, you freak.'

They heard the wail of the approaching sirens. The killer said, 'The real cops are coming. No time for sex. Take this.'

The sirens stopped when the cars were half a mile away.

And he shot at her. She flung to her left and took cover and shot in the direction of the killer. That man retreated in to shadows and was not visible. Other police cars screeched to a halt. The Police looked around, while Mary ran after the killer. The cops that arrived were six in number and there were three cars. One of the police men spotted Frank and ordered, 'Drop any weapon in your possession and get up with the hands raised.'

Frank was in a dilemma. If he gets up, he would be a sitting duck to the fugitive. If he does not, the police will shoot him. The blood drained out of his face. His face was ashen with fear. The other policemen too moved towards him. It was Frank against six policemen, who will be congratulated for killing the fugitive. The only difference was that he was not a fugitive and he was unarmed. They will realise their mistake only after his death. He sat up on his knees and raised his hands. One of the cops pointed a flash light at him. They saw Frank and did not see any gun.

'Where is the gun?' asked a cop.

'I don't have any weapon.'

'Then, stand up.'

Shots were fired here in the distance. Frank realised that the killer ran away with Mary in pursuit.

He slowly rose to his feet hands raised. 'Turn around slowly. If you as much as twitch, you are dead.'

Frank obeyed slowly. A cop came forward, pulled Frank's hands together at the back and hand cuffed him. They sent an all clear messages to the ambulance and clues team. They read his rights. The interrogation was painful in the sense that they were asking the same question over and over again, they asked, 'Who is the dead man? Where is your gun?'

After half an hour Mary rang up. They informed her that they have captured the killer. She was surprised, but was relieved. She thought that Frank must have left the scene safely.

When she came to the police station, she went straight to the interrogation room.

When she saw who was being questioned, she said loudly in exasperation, 'That is not the killer. He is Frank.'

'Good, but we are yet to see his frankness?'

'Frank is my boyfriend. We were returning home after dinner, when we came upon the murder. We surprised the killer, but he got away. I did not get a clear look at him.'

They apologised and released Frank.

Frank accused, 'You almost killed me.'

Archibald asked, 'Why didn't you tell them that you are Mary's boyfriend.'

'I did, but the officer thought that I was joking.'

'Why are you afraid? You should have asserted yourself.'

'The fugitive was firing at me. After him, the police were pointing their guns at me. Some body focused bright light on me, but only for a second. He could have known that I have no weapon.'

'A sharp shooter will fire at the light and could have got an officer.'

'Are you really her boyfriend?'

'Yes, I am her fiancé.'

'Congratulations. Mary did not tell me.'

'I proposed to her on the spur of the moment. I did not have a ring. We were going to announce it on Saturday.'

He was released by the police.

Archibald asked, 'Mary, you are going to marry him?'

'Yes. I was, until this incident. Now, I know that I can't marry him. Not anymore. He says that I am trigger happy.'

'He doesn't know how to handle such situations. He doesn't know that the best defence is counter offence. If you don't deal with such situations aggressively, you are most likely to end up as the victim.'

After his release, he went straight to his parents.

His mother was concerned. She asked, 'What happened? You look like a stricken man. I never saw you so white with fear. You appear to have had a dangerous encounter.'

Frank narrated his experience. 'Dad, I was shot at by a criminal who killed a man minutes before and the Police nearly killed me. Six police men pointed their guns at me. They demanded that I should drop my weapons and stand with hands raised. Slight movement by me like moving my toe in my shoe or change the level of the raised arm would provoke them to shoot.'

'Did Mary handle the situation confidently?'

'She did not bat an eye lid. She was not afraid. She took it in her stride. It was not courage. It was not an adventure. It was not a stray incident. It was routine. I looked at Death in the eye.'

His mom said, 'We are disappointed.'

'I still love her, but, I wonder if the marriage will work. I will become a nervous wreck.'

'Was she in her area of operation when she tackled the man with the gun?'

'No, she says that the police do not ignore a crime if it does not fall under their jurisdiction. They will act according to circumstances and pass on the case to the police in whose jurisdiction the case falls.'

'You must get out of this jinx regarding your girlfriends.'

MARY MILTON

Archibald said, 'Mary, listen to me. Marriage with Frank will not work. Think again. You were both lucky that this incident had taken place before your marriage.'

Mary replied, 'He is peeved with the interrogation. Nobody had believed his statement that he was my fiancé.'

'He was crawling on his elbows at the scene of the crime. He did not have a gun. It is not unusual. Nobody will believe him under the circumstances.'

Mary said, 'That kind of crimes and firing at the police are rare in our country, it may happen once in a life time.'

'Yes. When it happens that is the end of life time. Don't try to rationalise. It is your life and your decision. But as your friend, my advice is "get out of it."'

'I want to give it a try. He may get accustomed to life of fighting crime.'

'That is a fantasy. I do not understand what you see in him. The decision is yours.'

Frank asked Mary, 'Are you really interested in the police job?'

'Yes, that is my first love. I have always dreamed of becoming a police officer. The thrill and adventure are my life. You get involved in crime legally. Not that I want to commit a crime.'

'You fired your gun at that man as a matter of routine. It was not courage or adventure. You did not take cover until that man fired at you.'

'It is true, I was careless. But, you experience the authority of the police. I have arrested people using the gun by demanding it. They normally obey the authority of the police. Even if you don't have a gun most of the people surrender.'

'Can't you give up your job. You have to put in long hours, deal with criminals and violence and a difficult family life.'

'It is not like that. We get used to negative side of human nature, but it is service oriented.'

'It is true that police are service minded. I do not think that they have time for the family.'

Mary said, 'I enjoy the work. I am comfortable with life dealing with crime.'

Frank said, 'I hate admitting to you that the marriage with you may not work. I cannot live worrying about your safety. In a few months, I will become a nervous wreck.'

'I agree with you. It will be difficult to lead a life of peace and tranquillity. I think we better cancel the engagement.'

'Yes. Thank you for your love and affection. I regret that our relationship has come to an end this way.'

'Me too.'

Mary never regretted calling off the engagement. She also congratulated herself for not sleeping with Frank. Not that she did not want it, but they never got to it.

Frank said, 'Lucky that we did not make love. I regret the lack of opportunity but that is one confession less.'

Mary laughed and said, 'I missed it. We did not have the time.'

Frank's mother welcomed Mary with great affection. She said, 'I am pleased that you come to us to inform us about the cancellation of your marriage plans.'

Mary replied, 'We did not have a fight. We are both convinced that the marriage is not compatible.'

'That is great, marriage is more than love. If you are seeking love, you can live together without the responsibility, and the liability of marriage. Society has accepted that arrangement.'

'Mom, you are making marriage undesirable. The responsibility and the liability are nothing compared to the security and the joy of sharing life's adventures.'

'I did not mean it that way. I only told you that there is an alternative available. I do not want you to get into such arrangement.'

After some time, they dispersed. Next morning, she informed Archibald, 'We have broken off the engagement. I regret that the marriage with Frank did not work out. He is the most eligible bachelor.'

A few days later, Diana spotted Mary and Siva in a restaurant and walked to their table.

She said, 'Can I join you? I know that you are not dating, but meet frequently as friends.'

'That is the advantage with Siva. You can spend your time with him without feeling guilty or in anticipation of anything.'

Diana replied, 'He drinks very rarely and prefers vegetarian food. You can spend time with him comfortably.'

'Ladies, you are making me blush. As I am in London, I try to live like a Londoner. I have broken my tradition by eating chicken and mutton, even though rarely. Diana, please convey my regards to Sir Robert when you meet him.'

Diana replied, 'It is better if you meet him personally. You are treated with affection in that house. Don't lose contact.'

'Yes, I will keep in touch with him. I will ascertain from James, the butler, when it would be convenient for Sir Robert.'

'It is very difficult to get into that group of Sir Robert, Lady Kat, Ruth and Sally's mother. I am not part of their company but you are, thanks to Sally,' commented Mary.

Mary asked, 'Diana, are you married?'

'Yes, once. We broke off before the first anniversary of our wedding. Both of us wonder how we got married in the first place. The incompatibility was evident in the first month of our marriage.'

'Are you dating anybody?'

'No. I got the divorce about nine months back. I am not in a hurry. That experience is still rattling me. How is your date, Mary? I heard that you are engaged to Frank Miller.'

'No, that did not take off. The engagement is cancelled. Frank is now free. He has a jinx with girl friends.'

'What was wrong with him?'

'Nothing. He is gentle, educated with enviable career in a Bank. He is soft spoken, considerate and everything a woman asks for.'

'Why did you break up?'

'He cannot live with a wife who is a police woman. He cannot stand the violence and crime we are exposed to. His life will be miserable with worry and tension over her welfare.'

Frank walked in and joined them. 'I had a hunch that I will meet my friends here. Hello, Diana, It is lovely to meet you.' He nodded at Mary and Siva and settled down.

Mary and Siva got up to leave.

Frank asked, 'Are you leaving? Please spend a few more minutes with me. Otherwise, I will feel that you are leaving on account of me.'

They sat down. Siva said, 'I have to report for work at Eddie's in half an hour. I normally report for work half an hour or fifteen minutes early.'

Mary said, 'We have been here for over an hour.'

They spent a few minutes with Frank and left.

Frank asked, 'Diana, you are not in hurry to leave, no?'

'I am good for another hour. I am told that your engagement with Mary is blown.'

'Yes. Had she taken it badly?'

'No, she is all praise for you. She regrets that the engagement failed to take off.'

'She is a wonderful girl. When we were returning from a dinner date, we came across a man with a gun who killed a man minutes before. When she tried to apprehend him he took a shot at her. Later, he fired at me when I was crawling to safety. Police noticed me and threatened to shoot, if I do not surrender to them. I cannot live that kind of life with tension, and worry about her safety.'

'Mary is all praise for you. She says you are jinxed as far as girl friends are concerned.'

'Yes, I have been unlucky with girls. I was close to Sally since play school days. We grew up together and were spending a lot of time with each other. But, Sally does not love me. I did not impress Sundari. She is already engaged to a man living in India. Mary and I got a flying start, but I cannot live with the violence and crime in her job.'

They spoke for a long time and dispersed with a promise to meet again soon.

Mary walked into Starbucks in Staines to find Siva with a man she felt she knew but unable to place him. She joined them. Siva introduced Mary to Mark a soccer player. Her favourite sport is cricket and whenever she had time she would watch cricket or Rugby.

Siva is acquainted with Mark through his cousin, who is sharing his accommodation. Mark graduated in political science at age of 20. In his school days he was good at the game, but the school coach did not recognise his talent. In the college, he was encouraged with a scholarship. He was noted as talented. After graduation, he met the coach who gave him an opportunity to play in the intra national games. Slowly his game improved and he was hired by Real Madrid. He did not, however, get an opportunity to play in the club soccer or in the national team. Everybody believed that he has a career and a future in football.

Siva said, 'Mark, here, is a Soccer player and has chosen the game as his career. He is a promising professional. Mark, Mary here is a police woman in the Homicide Wing of the London Metropolitan Police.'

'Soccer is very popular. The players are paid fabulously and they are all rich,' commented Mary.

Mary wanted to spend some time with Siva. She did not call him but went in search of him at their favourite haunts. When she found him with another man, she went to them to spend some time with them. She was delighted to meet a professional football player. After a few minutes she left them and returned to the police station.

When Siva, Sally, Sundari and Diana came to their usual meeting place, the Starbucks, they started talking about their favourite subjects. That was not a prearranged meeting. One after another they came there in search of some company to while away their free time.

Sundari asked, 'Diana, you talked of debris some time back. Are we leaving an environmental disaster to the future generations?'

'It seems very likely. The only positive factor is that the depletion of Ozone layer is arrested. It has not grown. There is a lot more to do. Global warming is growing at an alarming rate. Climate is changing.'

When they were alone, Mark asked Siva, 'That police woman is beautiful. She must already have married or going to be married.'

'No, she is free.'

'With that kind of looks, if she is free, there must be something wrong with her.'

'No, she was engaged to a good looking banker. They cancelled the engagement two weeks ago.'

'Why did they break off?'

'There was some emotional incompatibility. He could not bear her duties. He was becoming a nervous wreck over her police duties. He was worrying about her safety. They are still friends.'

'Can I invite her for a date?'

'Yes, you can. Nobody can prevent you from taking her out, if she accepts. I don't see any reason why she would decline.'

'Great, is today's meeting enough to call her.'

'Why not? You did not take her phone number. You have to meet her again and take the number. I cannot give her number without her permission.'

'I think you are right.'

'I will arrange a meeting with her. It will appear to be casual.'

'Thank you.'

Meanwhile, Diana and Frank were going strong. They were meeting at least twice a week. There were instances of them meeting every day of the week. Frank started believing that she was his soul mate.

Siva asked Diana, Mary, Sally and Sundari if he could bring a friend to tea. They were reluctant at first, but finally agreed as a onetime event only. When they met on the next Saturday, Siva introduced Mark to the group. They knew Mark.

He is familiar. 'He is the future soccer star of Team GB. He has chosen football as his career and is doing well,' said Siva.

Mark replied, 'I can play very well. It all depends on my performance at the international level.'

'Are you confident about your capability?' asked Mary.

Mark was pleased. 'Yes. I am. After a couple of hours of discussion on various topics, they dispersed.

Before leaving Siva said, 'Mary, I want to say a few words to you.'

Mary said, 'I am listening.'

'Mark expressed interest in meeting you. Don't think that I am manipulating you. When he asked for your number, I told him that he had to take it from you, as I cannot give him the number without your permission. I invited him to today's meeting so that he can try his luck with you.'

'Thanks. He wanted me to go to dinner with him tomorrow. I gave him my number. He is very pleasant.'

'Good for you. Bye.'

Mark asked, 'Shall I drop you at your home?'

'I have my car.'

Siva asked, 'Mark, can I borrow your car. I will return it to you by 10 p.m.'

'Drop me at my place and take the car.'

Mary overheard this conversation and offered to give a lift to Mark. Mark accepted.

Mark said, 'I am not in the mood to go home for dinner. I want to dine out. Will you join me.'

'Yes. I am not in the mood to go home and cook my dinner. Let's go to an Indian restaurant in Houston. I developed a taste for the Indian curry and roti, thanks to Siva.'

'Indian food is my choice too.'

That was the first of their many dates over a period of three months.. They were meeting whenever Mark was in London. He was away in Europe waiting for his opportunity. They were going steady. Both of them discussed their hazardous occupations. They were prepared to face the challenges of life together.

One day, Archibald commented, 'You are going steady with Mark, the footballer?'

'Yes.'

'It may lead to marriage?'

'Yes.'

'I saw him playing football. He has talent. He is going to be a celebrity and famous. He has riches coming his way.'

'Yes. I am aware of that.'

'Once he becomes a celebrity and a great footballer, he is likely to be poached.'

'What are you trying to tell? That I may lose him to a beautiful and fashionable girl?'

'Yes. I have seen the WAGs. They are tough competition.'

'I will cross the river when I come to it. Thanks for your interest.'

'I am very possessive about you. I care for you and wish you well.'

'We haven't talked about marriage yet. But I can sense the proposal coming. There are many football players who married middle class girls. Your fears about poaching are baseless. It is my fate if it happens. I will take it in my stride'

A week after this conversation, Mark returned to London and met Mary.

'Mary, I have something serious to tell you.'

'What is it?'

'I love you. I want to marry you. Before proposing, I want to tell you that I am likely to be injured in my career. Barring a couple of incidents worldwide there were no fatal injuries. I will be away for long spells playing in tournaments. That is all I wanted to tell you.'

He kneeled and asked, 'Mary, will you marry me?'

Mary said, 'Before considering your proposal, I wish to tell you seriously, that I am likely to be injured and on rare occasions, fatally. I may come home late or leave home at nights on Police Business. I slept with a boyfriend on a couple of occasions before breaking it off.'

'The nature of our duties is widely known. There is nothing new, but it had to be explained. I understand your situation. Will you please marry me?'

'Yes'. He slipped the diamond ring on her finger and kissed her.

Next evening, they went to Mary's home. Her parents received him with great pleasure. Mary's mother was overwhelmed with delight. They were impressed with Mark. They celebrated the occasion with champagne and excellent dinner. Mark's parents were equally delighted with the news.

Mark's dad said 'You are both very young. You have a long and happy married life ahead. When do you intend to marry?'

'As soon as arrangements for marriage are made. We are short of money right now. We are confident that we will make arrangements in a couple of months.'

'We will also chip in. Youngsters have selected their spouses. As parents we will support you. There is no way we can give you any money after the marriage. Select an event manager and we will discuss the cost and the means to meet it.'

Mary's parents invited Mark's parents for dinner. When they were all together, they discussed the wedding.

Mary's mother said, 'The children are very young and yet to make a comfortable living. We are prepared to meet part cost of the event. I have the bridal suit from my wedding. It smells of Naphthalene balls, but a laundry can make it smell better and look better.'

'Will the children accept that,' asked Mark's mother

'I will convince them. What will they do with a new bridal attire which she will wear for a few hours only. That money can be used for another necessity.'

'As I have to give the bride away, it will be my privilege to share the cost.'

They contacted an Event Manager who agreed to arrange the wedding for 30,000 pounds, but the wedding date is 9 months away.

Mark's father said, 'There are several boys and girls who are living together, have babies and not married. The reason is that they don't have money for the wedding'

'Marriage is no problem. You can marry at the government marriage registry and solemnise the wedding in the Christian tradition. This is expensive. You should invite all your friends and the relatives to the marriage. It is most likely that you forget to invite somebody, and face their hurt and anger. It happens in every wedding. I am happy that you have agreed to share the cost.'

Mark said, 'You are treating us like children.'

'You are.'

Mary said, 'Why should you spend your money on our marriage, we will bear the expenses. I have 6,000/- pounds, as savings. I can borrow another 4,000/- pounds, I have 10,000/- pounds.'

Mark said that he can contribute 6,000/- pounds.

Mary's Dad said 'I have set aside 15,000/- pounds for her marriage. It may not be enough for her today. But that is available.'

Mark's dad said, 'I can contribute 15,000/- pounds. The aggregate amount should be adequate.'

Mary's mother signalled to Mary to come into the kitchen and said, 'I will bring some more coffee' and went into the kitchen.

She asked, 'Mary did you discuss your boy friends with Mark. Be frank and confess if you slept with anyone. If you tell him now it will be forgiven in the euphoria.'

'Mom, my first boyfriend was Siva. Siva is handsome, light in colour and an engineering graduate from India. He came from India to pursue his post graduate studies in Space sciences. After Siva, Frank was my friend. Then came Mark.'

'Did you sleep with any of them?'

'With Frank, we did not have time to engage in sex. We were good friends but didn't get the opportunity.'

'What about Siva?'

'Yes, I slept with Siva a couple of times. Then we stopped as we felt that our marriage would be a disaster.'

'Did Siva report this to Mark.'

'No, he says it is for me to tell him. He cannot tell him as Mark will look askance at me. He says that Mark will feel that he was cheated. I told Mark that I am not a virgin.'

'That is not enough. Tell him frankly and honestly. If he doesn't accept you then he isn't suitable to you. You avoid the trauma of your marriage breaking up.'

'Your advice is excellent. I will certainly settle the matter. Thank you. I am proud of you.'

On the way home she told him, 'Mark, I told you that I am not a virgin. I didn't give you the details. I dated Siva. He was my first boyfriend. I slept with him twice. We realised that it's not practical and we will not be happy together.'

'Why didn't Siva tell me about it.'

'Siva is not marrying you. He can't tell you without knowing if I intend to inform you.'

'Very well. I am impressed about your honesty. I don't care about life before the marriage but please be truthful and committed to the marriage. I will not cheat on you. I am not a virgin either. I had sex with four girls. They were anxious to give it away. There is nothing to it.'

'My, you are a Casanova.'

'My Coach said that I was promiscuous. I am leading a life that is devoid of moral and social sensitivity. Continuation of this kind of life will ruin me.'

Mary said 'I am relieved of my tension. I am grateful that you took it with such grace and abandon.'

'There is nothing I can do about what happened in the past. I look forward to a happy life with you. I will live my life as my coach advised me. I will concentrate on my career. I will stay true to our vows.'

'So do I.'

SIVA

Two weeks later, Diana and Frank announced their engagement. Their marriage was one year away. They were not concerned about the expenses. Frank's parents heaved a sigh of relief. His dad said, 'I have my fingers crossed. I will celebrate when the wedding is over.'

Frank's mother said; 'He was unlucky with girlfriends. He has overcome the situation. They will marry and live happily.'

In their group only Siva and Sally were without girl or boy friends.

Sally commented, 'I am the only one without a fiancé or boyfriend.'

Sally and Sundari were sitting in the Subway.

Sundari said, 'You are good looking and rich. It is a surprise that you have no boyfriends. Its perhaps because you are the most eligible girl. The boys must be shying away because of the millions you are going to inherit and that they cannot hope to match you.'

'If that is the case, I will end up a spinster.'

'You are demoralised. You will get your man. Don't panic.'

Sally's phone rang. It was from Siva.

He asked, 'Sally, I am going to meet your mother. Are you at home.'

'No, I and Sundari are in the Subway.'

'Why don't you both come with me.'

'You go ahead we will join you. We are on our way.'

They arrived at Ms. Richard's house at the same time. They were invited into the house.

Sundari commented, 'Sally is worried. She thinks that she will end up a spinster.'

'That's rubbish. She will find her man. She's still young. There is plenty of time for her.'

Siva said, 'She is in love with a man. She does not realise it.'

'Who is that?'

'I don't know. It was Frank's observation.'

'It must be Don. But that's past. She must have another man.'

Ms. Richard asked, 'Siva, why don't you talk about Space. You explain the complicated Cosmic matters in a simple language for a lay man.'

It was clear that she didn't want to talk about Sally's marriage.

'Thank you. I am interested in breaking the barriers to space travel.'

'What are the barriers?'

'The distances. I think that man has to identify other dimensions of four and more. In three dimensional world, we cannot reach the other planets. Man should invent glasses to see four or more dimensions converted to three dimensional vision.'

'Do you think life exists in another planet?'

'In the billions of galaxies and stars life must be existing. Earth cannot be the only planet with life. Have you seen the movie, "Predator?" Hero was Arnold Schwarzenegger. It was fiction of course but the creature who was predating could exist, in other dimensions. The flying saucers are another possibility. I don't remember the name of the movie, but it shows dogs from another planet. At present man's ability to break the barriers of three dimensions appear to be light years away.'

'You think that creatures from other planets visit the Earth.'

'That's possible if such creatures are technologically superior. Then they would colonise earth.'

'Do you think that the dreams of fiction writers are achievable?'

'I think it's a possibility even though remote. Man dreamed and made it a reality, but I wonder if we can break the cosmic barriers.'

Sundari said 'Daina feels that man is ruining the Earth. It will not attract the aliens.'

Ms. Richard asked 'Why don't you and Sundari call Diana, DI.'

'We are influenced by our mother tongue. You call Diana Dee but in Telugu the letter I is pronounced as in "time". Instead of calling her Dee, we may inadvertently call her Die.'

When they met again, Siva asked, 'Frank, you told us that Sally was in love but does not realise it. Who is it?'

'I don't have to spell it. It is writing on the wall.'

Sundari said, 'I think that I can read the writing on the wall..'

'Who is that?'

'I think that I should wait for some more time.'

'That is no help.'

Siva was in a dilemma. He realised that his education in London would not get him a job. There are some more British citizens in his class who will get priority over him. In U.K. you can't get a job without experience. He should return to India gain some experience and seek employment and return. Archibald was right. He could get a job in India with his engineering degree. But his thirst for the knowledge of Space made him pursue the study of Space sciences. Space research is not confined to one discipline. It requires engineers in other disciplines and sciences. He made friends with exceptional persons in London who could be friends for life. He loved London and loved its people. They are ready to smile. They have a positive approach to life. He realised that he should learn from the Londoners, cultivate their positive attitude. He was jerked out of his reflections by the ring of his mobile. The call was from Sally.

'Can you come to the Starbucks? I want to talk to you.'

'Others may also come there.'

'That is alright.'

When he reached the place he found her sipping coffee.

Sundari and Diana entered and approached them and settled down on the vacant chairs at their table.

Diana asked, 'Are we interrupting?'

'No. you are both welcome. We are past the stage of interruption and apology. You can join us any time.'

Siva said, 'I was about to tell Sally that I fell for her at first sight.'

Sally laughed, 'He fell because I kicked him on the face. That was how we met for the first time.'

'That is funny. But I think that he really fell for you.'

'That is not funny. I paid him the damages.'

'You got away with a small payment. He could have extracted a lot more from you. The Judges don't take the physical assault lightly. They award heavy compensation for the injury. They may also send the attacker to jail. The invisible damages like pain, agony etc., will be treated with harsh penalties,' commented Diana.

Sundari said, 'You have been taking care of him. You snub him when he tries to flatter you. You tell him that he was dark and that it wouldn't happen.'

'I don't know how it would affect me if I lose my virginity. I don't want to throw it away. I realise that I was protecting myself from him. Siva take my comments lightly,' said Sally.

Siva said, 'That is alright. I was never offended by your comments.'

'My friendship with Don convinced me that virginity is not something you throw away. There is an element of moral conviction and the natural selection. I am not guilty of being unfair to Siva.'

Sundari said, 'We agree. Diana and I are going to a flower show in Hampton Court. Will you join us?'

'You go ahead. We'll spend some time and go.'

Sundari asked Diana, 'Did you read the writing on the wall.'

'I did. Long time back. Strange that she did not realise it.'

Sally asked, 'Siva, are you a one woman man?'

'Yes.'

'Good.'

'One woman at a time.'

'I am disappointed.'

'I lost my virginity or bachelorhood with two women. You can't resist the women in London.'

On their way, Sundari commented, 'It is not easy for Siva to marry Sally. There are hurdles.'

'What are they?'

'His Visa. He came to London on a student visa. To get work permit he has to return to India, gain some experience and find an employer in London. It may take one or two years. Sally has to live in India with him until he gets a job in London.'

'What is the problem?'

'Will Sally accept that? Siva is from a middle class family. The standard of living in the middle class is not as high as in London. She is a millionaire. Siva can't survive a divorce.'

'Why do you talk about divorce even before the proposal.'

'You have to consider all the aspects. I have plans for Siva.'

'I am told that you have a fiancé in India.'

'That is right. But I have plans for him. He has the qualities of an entrepreneur. I want to use him.'

Diana said, 'They are made for each other. They don't have to date and go steady. They meet every day. Sally loves him. They should both realise their feelings towards each other.'

'Earlier the better.'

'Sally takes care of Siva and was very protective about him.'

Sally told her mother, 'Mom, I want to talk to you.'

'What about?'

'I think I am in love with Siva.'

'Congratulations for this revelation. It was written all over your face. Why do you think I was inviting Siva to our home. He said that you consider him dark and unfit for you. Nobody in London will talk to him like that. We are too civil. I think that you are subconsciously resisting you infatuation with him.'

'He will not get a job in U.K. without experience. He should return to India and get some experience and look for a job in London.'

'What is your problem? There is nothing wrong with India. It was the jewel of the British Empire. It is a wonderful place. It is hot but an incredible country. Spending a few years in India will be good for you. You can visit all the important places, while you are there. Siva is your man. Go and take possession.'

'Thank you. I am not worried about leaving London. It is only twelve hours from here.'

'Sally, you are a wonderful person. Siva will propose to you. I noticed that he loves you. That is why I ask him to visit me.'

'Mom, you seem to be in love with him.'

'Yes. I adore him like my son. Don't have any misgivings.'

'Mom, I am sorry that you got the impression that I don't approve your meeting Siva.'

'We look down on the Indians and consider them inferior to us. Shakespeare wrote that "there is a tide in the affairs of men." It is true in the case of nations too. Krishna delivered the Geeta in Aug 3129 B.C.'

'Mom, you have done considerable research about Siva's language and culture.'

'I love my daughter. I will not allow my daughter to marry in to civilisations that do not treat their women well. Indians suffered subordination for 800 years. First by the Muslims and later by the British. The English arrived and recognised the Muslim rulers. This helped the Muslim rulers. The Hindu sages were raising Indian armies to fight the Muslim rulers.

The British did not understand the Hindu culture. They were shocked by the Hindu reverence of sex and their worship of phallic symbols. They ignored the Hindu philosophy and their culture. They could not imagine the history beyond five thousand years.' 'Mom, it is true that I love Siva. Can I spend my life away from London forever?'

'If you go to India for the sake of living with him, we can persuade him to come to London.'

'How long will it be.'

'Two to four years.'

'Siva should propose.'

Sally called Siva. He said that he would be at Starbucks or Subway in half an hour. Sally was worried as Siva never raised the topic of love or marriage. Her comments about Siva being dark and that he had no chance of making it made him hesitate to propose. But he will propose even if he felt that it would not be accepted.

Siva said, 'I am leaving in another four to six months. I enjoyed my stay in London, especially the friendship with you. We made friends with good and intelligent people. I will cherish the memories of my life in London. It is a wonderful country with wonderful people.'

'You are bidding farewell?'

'No. There is time. I am nervous and fidgety about the memories of London which are coming to an end soon.'

Sally realised that it is coming. She was afraid that she may blow it with her stupid comments.

'Sally, listen I cannot postpone it any longer. I love you. I want to marry you. But there are hurdles. In spite of my infatuation with you, I can't propose to you.'

'You have taken your sweet time to say that you love me. I am on cloud nine. What are the hurdles?'

'I can't be permanent resident of London by marrying its citizen. I have to leave this country in few months. I want to make love to you if I can't marry you. I want to leave London with pleasant memories. You kicked me on the face, called me dark and that I can't hope to have sex with you. But I love you.'

'You are very smart. You cannot propose to me but can proposition to me.'

'Yes. I want it only if I can't continue in London.'

'That is fair. Let us try to solve your problem of visa. If all our efforts fail, I will give you what you want.'

'That is torture. Both of us are willing. Why do you procrastinate. How can a man live in perpetual anticipation.'

'If we can't overcome this situation, I will live with you in India.'

Siva jumped in joy. He asked Sally to stand up. When she did, he kneeled and said,

'Sally Richards, I am madly in love with you. I beg you. Will you marry me?'

'Siva Kanuri, yes. I will marry you. It will be my privilege and pleasure. I see that you don't have a ring. Slip it on later.'

The diners in the restaurant clapped and congratulated them.

The owner of the restaurant said, 'We are delighted that our restaurant has brought two persons together into matrimony. Your dinner and drinks are on the house.'

'Can we sleep together now?'

'No. Let us solve the problem.'

'I slept with two women.'

'Why do you keep on repeating it. You already told me. I don't care. I am not interested in knowing those women.'

They discussed their predicament with their friends. They considered several alternatives which were not feasible.

Sundari walked in. She was surprised to see them all in furious discussion. When she sat down, Diana informed, 'Siva proposed to Sally. She accepted.'

'Congratulations to them.. Everyone could see that they were madly in love with each other, except the two of them.'

Mary said, 'There is a problem.'

'What is it?'

'Siva has to leave in a few months.'

'Siva can't get a job without experience. If he can't return to London, The marriage is not viable.'

'What is the big deal? If he can't return to London, Sally will go to India.'

'What about the family business.'

'What about the business. They are not running those businesses. They are managed by professionals. They only instruct the managers and set the targets for business. They can do that from India.'

'What about the cultural incompatibility?'

'There is nothing wrong with India. It is a free country. The middle class is catching up with the West in the standard of living. In London, people consider the Indians inferior. That is absurd. In the Middle East and India people eat with their fingers. That is their culture. There is nothing wrong with it. The Indians are touring the South East Asia, Europe and other countries. They spend money in travel. That is business. They lived in isolation and paid the price.' 'So, what do you suggest?'

'If Siva can't stay in London, She should go to India. I have plans for Siva. Siva is skilled in Software. He says he doesn't have experience. I have seen him work. He has communication skills. I want to set up a business in India. Siva will be the Chairman and Managing Director. My husband and I will be on the Board. We will invest in the business.'

'Will it be successful?'

'Yes. We will work hard and make it a success. After two years or more, we will open the British arm of the company in London. We will invest money and create jobs. We should open our office in U.S. first. But in view of their marriage, we will open the London branch. Siva will move to London Office. I am not doing any favour to Sally or Siva. It is cold blooded logic. I have no doubt that it will soon be a major player in the market.'

Diana said, 'Sundari, you are a genius. I have seen that you analyse situations and find a solution to a problem.'

It is true. But my analysis could be wrong. As it is my habit, I have set a few parameters to select a business. They are,

1. It should be sophisticated technology and only we can manufacture or create the product,
2. It should require minimum investment in plant and machinery,
3. It should be highly profitable,
4. It should have demand globally.'

'Are there any such companies.' asked Mary.

'Yes. It is only the first parameter that is difficult. Siva can take the challenge. He should travel extensively and acquire expertise in the Space Sciences.'

'How much will be required as initial investment?'

'It will be very low. What I propose is a software company. We will market our services, get an order and ask for an advance. We will, take a sick software company on lease and commence operations. But that will force us to lead a hand to mouth existence. Any unforeseen situation may result in the collapse of the company. We will start with initial small equity.'

Sally informed her mother and Sir Robert about Sundari's plan. Ms. Richard was delighted and could not find words to express her happiness. She and Sir Robert were considering the ways of bringing Siva to London. Sundari solved the problem.

She told Sally, 'Let them start their business.. Sir Robert and I will take care of that company. Your marriage to Siva has no hurdles. In India three generations live together. The parents, the adult son and his wife and his children. In London, we will live together. I can't leave you. I want to live with my grandchildren. The house is big and we have the money.'

Sir Robert said, 'Sally, You are going to Telugu speaking state in India. It has continuous literary activity for the last thousand years. An Englishman compiled and published the first Telugu Dictionary. Telugu is rich in classical music and dance. Try to learn it. People will respect you and treat you with affection. During the British rule, the currency and coins were in English and inevitably Telugu. Bengali, Urdu and Hindi were tried one after the other. I love India and am interested in it in view of our association with it.'

Lady Kat commented, 'Everybody is talking of Sally's marriage. Did anybody think of Siva's parents? Siva can't ignore his parents. If they are not happy, Siva will not be happy.'

That afternoon Ms. Richard called Siva's. parents. She said, 'I am calling from London. I am Sally's mother. Siva must have explained that Sally and he are engaged.'

'Yes. He told us about his plans for the marriage. We are pleased. Congratulations. We are gaining a daughter and not losing a son. We will not come in the way of his happiness. The family bonds are strong in India. We want to see our daughter-in-.law. We want them to marry in the Hindu tradition. If they want to marry in India, we will meet all the expenses. But you should give us reasonable time. If they can't come to India, we will come to London.'

Ms. Richard agreed to their requirements and promised to get back to them. She was willing to accept every thing they asked.

Siva met her next evening. He said, 'My dad called me and informed me about your call. They are applying for a Visa. They should be treated well. I told them that I am returning to India. I have a sister living in India. She is also coming. They are excited about the wedding.'

The wedding was two months away as it can be held in the campus of Sally's house which has a large open space and big house.

Sir Robert and Ms. Richard invited Sundari for dinner at Sir Robert's house. During dinner, Sir Robert asked, 'How much is the initial investment in the proposed Software Company. How do you propose to raise it?'

Sundari replied, 'Initially, we propose to contribute one grand each. That will be four thousand pounds, approximately Rupees 360,000/- If we need more, we will contribute another thousand pounds each. It will be a closely held company with four directors. They are Siva, Sally, my fiancé and I.'

Sir Robert stared at her and said, 'That is peanuts. In case you need any further amounts please tell us. We are good for a million pounds each or more. Four thousand pounds is not an investment.'

'Thank you. We will keep your offer in mind. I will manage the finances of the Company. The major investment of the company is the intellectual property.'

Printed in the United States
By Bookmasters